A Candlelight Ecstasy Romance®

"YOU'RE GOING BACK TO MARSHALL?" DARCY DEMANDED.

"Yes," Glory answered softly, forcing herself not to flinch from the contempt in his eyes.

"Now I know why you wouldn't let me announce our engagement. You were gambling that Marshall would want you back. And if that didn't work out I was supposed to be the consolation prize." Darcy shook his head in deep disgust. "You could have made a fortune as an actress if you'd wanted to work for money instead of marrying for it. When I think of all those nights you spent in my arms declaring your undying love—I realize now I should have applauded."

Tears welled up in Glory's eyes. "I'm sorry you feel betrayed," she began, "but let me explain."

"There's no need," Darcy said contemptuously. "I think we've covered everything."

Be sure to read this month's
CANDLELIGHT ECSTASY CLASSIC ROMANCES . . .

THE TAWNY GOLD MAN, *Amii Lorin*
GENTLE PIRATE, *Jayne Castle*

CANDLELIGHT ECSTASY ROMANCES®

442 FEVER PITCH,
Pamela Toth

443 ONE LOVE
FOREVER,
Christine King

444 WHEN LIGHTNING
STRIKES,
Lori Copeland

445 WITH A LITTLE
LOVE,
Natalie Stone

446 MORNING GLORY,
Donna Kimel Vitek

447 TAKE-CHARGE
LADY,
Alison Tyler

448 ISLAND OF
ILLUSIONS,
Jackie Black

449 THE PASSIONATE
SOLUTION,
Jean Hager

QUANTITY SALES

Most Dell Books are available at special quantity discounts when purchased in bulk by corporations, organizations, and special-interest groups. Custom imprinting or excerpting can also be done to fit special needs. For details write: Dell Publishing Co., Inc., 1 Dag Hammarskjold Plaza, New York, NY 10017, Attn.: Special Sales Dept., or phone: (212) 605-3319.

INDIVIDUAL SALES

Are there any Dell Books you want but cannot find in your local stores? If so, you can order them directly from us. You can get any Dell book in print. Simply include the book's title, author, and ISBN number, if you have it, along with a check or money order (no cash can be accepted) for the full retail price plus 75¢ per copy to cover shipping and handling. Mail to: Dell Readers Service, Dept. FM, P.O. Box 1000, Pine Brook, NJ 07058.

NO GREATER LOVE

Jan Stuart

A CANDLELIGHT ECSTASY ROMANCE®

Published by
Dell Publishing Co., Inc.
1 Dag Hammarskjold Plaza
New York, New York 10017

Copyright © 1986 by Jan Stuart

All rights reserved. No part of this book may be reproduced or transmitted in any form or by any means, electronic or mechanical, including photocopying, recording, or by any information storage and retrieval system, without the written permission of the Publisher, except where permitted by law.

Dell ® TM 681510, Dell Publishing Co., Inc.

Candlelight Ecstasy Romance®, 1,203,540, is a registered trademark of Dell Publishing Co., Inc., New York, New York.

ISBN: 0-440-16377-3

Printed in the United States of America

August 1986

10 9 8 7 6 5 4 3 2 1

WFH

To Our Readers:

We have been delighted with your enthusiastic response to Candlelight Ecstasy Romances®, and we thank you for the interest you have shown in this exciting series.

In the upcoming months we will continue to present the distinctive sensuous love stories you have come to expect only from Ecstasy. We look forward to bringing you many more books from your favorite authors and also the very finest work from new authors of contemporary romantic fiction.

As always, we are striving to present the unique, absorbing love stories that you enjoy most—books that are more than ordinary romance. Your suggestions and comments are always welcome. Please write to us at the address below.

Sincerely,

The Editors
Candlelight Romances
1 Dag Hammarskjold Plaza
New York, New York 10017

NO GREATER LOVE

CHAPTER ONE

The cold, wet wind blowing in off the Pacific whipped Glory Wentworth's long red hair into damp tendrils around her pale face. The sand in her shoes was mixed with tiny shells that cut painfully into her high instep. She glanced down in bewilderment, wondering what she was doing walking on the beach in high-heeled sandals.

When a sudden gusty breeze drove the dark clouds away from the moon, she could see houses on a hill overlooking the stormy sea. They were large, brooding structures set far apart from each other, turning blank faces to the restless water. Only one house showed a light.

Where was this place? Was she having a nightmare? Glory felt panic rising in her throat as she realized that she didn't know how she had gotten there. The last thing she remembered was sitting in her sister's living room. Carole had been lecturing her about something. Carole! Glory started to tremble uncontrollably at the realization that she knew her sister's name but not her own!

She tried to force down the panic. It would come to her. If only her head didn't ache so. She ran slender fingers through her silky hair, trying to think. Perhaps the people in that house above would help.

As she climbed the narrow wooden flight of steps up from the beach Glory was beset by further fears. Maybe they wouldn't even answer the door. A glance at her watch showed it was almost one o'clock in the morning. That was awfully late, and people were so wary now.

Her anxiety, on that score at least, was unwarranted. Almost as soon as she removed her shaking finger from the bell, the door was thrown open. A tall man with broad shoulders filled the entry. His back was to the light, so she couldn't tell anything about him except his height.

"Yes? Who is it?" The low masculine voice was slightly impatient.

"I—I—" Glory couldn't get any further, not knowing where to begin.

The lamplight flooded her face, illuminating the wide, frightened emerald eyes shaded by thick lashes that were black against the pallor of her flawless skin. As he looked at her parted trembling mouth, the man drew in his breath sharply.

His hand on her arm brought Glory inside, where she got her first look at him. He appeared to be in his middle thirties and was darkly handsome. His golden brown eyes glowed like a hungry lion's—or maybe it was just a reflection from the fireplace. Glory hoped that was it. He was formidable looking.

A black sweater hugged his powerful shoulders and chest, while tight jeans emphasized the narrowness of his hips and the lean length of his muscular thighs. Curling black hair showed through the vee neck of the pullover. As he regarded her the frown on his tanned face pulled dark brows together over a straight nose and a wide, generous mouth. The only reassuring thing about him were the laugh lines that hinted at a lighter side.

"What are you doing here at this time of night?" he demanded.

Glory's small white teeth tried to stop the quivering of her lower lip. "I—yours was the only light on."

His frown deepened. "That isn't what I asked. Who are you?"

She searched desperately for the answer, encountering only a blank wall. Terror threatened to swamp her. How did she get here? *She couldn't remember.*

The big man watched the play of emotions over her delicate face, his expression changing from one of suspicion to one of concern. "Are you all right?"

She gazed up at him, her soft mouth tremulous. "I don't know who I am."

He stared at her incredulously for a moment before her obvious distress convinced him. "Come over to the fire," he said gently. "You're cold."

Glory trailed obediently after him, sinking down on a large ottoman. In a kind of daze, she watched the play of muscles across the wide triangle of his back as he poked up the fire.

"There, that's better." He got to his feet, the tight jeans molding his powerful thighs. "Now for a drink to warm you inside as well as out." A smile showed even white teeth. He turned and walked toward the kitchen.

Glory stared down at her lap, smoothing the folds of her beige skirt with nervous fingers. She wore a short matching beige jacket and a jade green silk blouse with a soft bow at the neck. It was an outfit she had paid a great deal of money for. How did she know that when she couldn't even think of her own name? A terrible thought hit her. Sometimes people blanked out things too horrible to remember. Had she committed some awful crime? The panic was back in her eyes when the man returned with a bottle of brandy and two glasses on a tray.

"Where is this place?" she asked over the tightness in her throat.

"You're in Malibu." He poured amber liquid into a snifter. "Let me introduce myself," he offered casually. "I'm Darcy Lord."

"How do you do?" she answered automatically. "I'm—" Glory came up against a blank wall. "I—" Her eyes were agonized.

"Just relax and don't worry about it," he said easily. "It will come to you."

"Do you think so?" She grasped desperately at the hope he extended. "It's so awful not knowing." Her shaking fingers swept the cloud of red hair off her pale forehead.

Darcy gave a sharp exclamation, cupping her chin in his hand so he could examine her face. "Where did you get that gash on your forehead?"

"I . . . I don't know."

"You must have been in an accident." He touched her cheek very lightly. "You have the start of a black and blue mark here." He looked at her intently. "Can you remember being in a car?"

She shook her head. "That couldn't be it. I was walking along the beach."

Rage flared briefly in his eyes as he noticed other bruises on her neck. "Did you meet anyone?" His voice was carefully offhand.

"I don't know," she replied hopelessly.

"Well, it isn't important." He drew her to her feet. "The first order of business is to get you to the emergency hospital."

"What for? There's nothing wrong with me!"

"That cut has to be treated."

"No!" Glory wasn't fooled by his soothing tone. He wasn't taking her to a hospital. They put people like her in an institution, didn't they? She could almost feel the walls closing in! Pulling away from him, she made a dash for the door.

He caught her easily, holding her hands when she tried to strike out at him. "Hey, wait a minute. What's wrong?"

"Let go of me! I'm not going anywhere with you. I

don't want to be locked up like a stray animal." Tears streamed down her cheeks as she struggled wildly.

Darcy folded her in his arms, pressing her head against his solid shoulder as he stroked the gleaming mass of her silky hair. "No one is going to lock you up, honey. Where did you get a silly idea like that?"

The security of his arms was a seduction she had to fight against. Glory wanted to relax against this big man and shift her troubles to his broad shoulders. He seemed so capable, so understanding. It could be a trap, though, a ploy to get her to go quietly. Maybe he even thought she was crazy. What if I am? Glory thought wildly.

"Listen to me." Darcy's arm supported her while he raised her chin, then looked directly into her shadowed emerald eyes. "You've had a shock that has left you frightened and confused. That's understandable, but you musn't let it throw you. We're going to find out who you are, and everything is going to be fine. I won't let anything happen to you."

She was afraid to believe him. "Why would you bother? You don't even know me."

His golden brown eyes held hers. "I don't need to know you. You're in trouble. If we can't help each other, what's it all about?"

His quiet words helped to allay Glory's panic. As she followed him outside to the sleek sports car parked beside the house she felt her tension lifting. At least she wasn't alone in this nightmare any longer.

The emergency hospital was in a small building off the highway. The young doctor on duty was thorough and gentle and treated Glory's cuts and bruises with practiced efficiency. It was only when he found out about her loss of memory that trouble arose.

"There isn't anything here serious enough to have caused your trauma. You'll need X rays and neurological tests." He finished taping a small bandage to her forehead. "I don't have that equipment here; you'll have

13

to go to the hospital. Mercy Memorial will take care of you." He reached for the phone.

"No!" This was what Glory had been afraid of.

The doctor looked at her in surprise. "It won't be anything painful."

She turned to Darcy, whose face was full of concern. "You need help," he told her.

Bitterness filled her. What a fool she had been to trust this man! She measured the distance to the door. Edging toward it, she said, "Thank you, doctor, and you, too, Mr. Lord. You don't have to worry about me anymore. I'll be all right now."

The doctor moved quickly, cutting off her escape. "I can't let you leave here in this condition."

"You have no right to stop me!"

"Actually, it's a case for the police," the young medic said hesitantly.

"I haven't done anything!" Glory cried.

Hearing the ragged edge of hysteria in her voice, Darcy took over. He put his arm protectively around her shoulders. "What this young woman needs more than anything at the moment is a good night's rest. It's very possible that she'll be fine by morning."

The doctor looked doubtful. "Well, it's possible, of course, but—"

"I'll take her home with me," Darcy broke in firmly. "Tomorrow will be plenty of time to contact the authorities if it's necessary."

The other man looked at his watch. "It *is* pretty late, and I did give her something to make her sleep." He shook some pills out of a bottle, then put them in a small envelope, which he handed to Darcy. "Maybe you'd better take these just in case she needs calming down."

A small part of Glory was indignant, at being treated as though she were feebleminded, but she was too happy to be getting out of there to voice any protests.

After she was safely inside the car, Glory sighed, putting her head back against the leather seat. Reaction was setting in, making her inexpressibly weary. She watched Darcy's large, capable hands on the wheel. His fingers were long and tapered, with short, well-kept nails.

For the first time, Glory felt a twinge of curiosity about this man who had rescued her. What kind of work did he do? Why was he living way out here? Malibu was a beach community outside of Los Angeles. It was an exclusive area, populated mainly by the rich and famous. Why did she know all these unimportant things but not the one that mattered the most?

When she moved restlessly in her seat, Darcy said soothingly, "We're almost there. You must be exhausted."

"No . . . I . . . I was just thinking about things."

His warm hand covered hers. "Let it go for tonight. That's what I always do when things threaten to boil over."

"You look like you could handle any situation," she told him simply.

Darcy laughed. "Don't you believe it. My palms have sweated many a time when I was waiting for a jury to bring in its verdict."

"You're an attorney?"

He nodded. "With the firm of Bagley, Avondale, Suffolk and Lord."

"Don't you find it difficult to live this far from downtown Los Angeles?" she asked.

"It would be, on an everyday basis," he agreed. "Much as I love it here, I only get to use the house on weekends—or very occasionally during the week if I really need to get away."

Glory's eyes were luminous in the moonlight. "Is this . . . What day is today?"

"It's Saturday night." He looked at his watch. "Well, Sunday morning now."

"I've kept you up all night," she said remorsefully. "I hope you don't have any early morning plans."

"Just some briefs I have to prepare—and a couple of speeches to write." He laughed. "I welcome any opportunity to put that off."

"What kind of speeches?"

"Probably very dull ones," he replied deprecatingly.

"I don't believe that for a moment. Where are you going to deliver them?"

"During my campaign. I'm running for the state senate." In spite of his offhand manner, there was a quiet pride in his statement.

"How wonderful! Is your . . ." She wanted to ask him if his wife was helping him, but that sounded as though she were trying to find out if he were married. "I imagine your family is very proud of you," she substituted instead.

"Outside of a few cousins, I don't have any family." He shrugged. "It's probably just as well. If I fall on my face, I won't embarrass anyone except myself."

Glory gave him a little smile. "If I ever find out who I am, you have my vote."

"Don't make idle promises, lady," he teased. "In a day or two you'll be back to normal, and I'm going to hold you to it."

"It's a deal." She stared at him curiously. "You must be quite well known to be running for office."

He passed it off modestly. "I've had a few well-publicized cases."

"Tell me about them."

"They weren't all that interesting. I just helped to make a couple of giant corporations responsible for their actions." There was a look of satisfaction on his strong face.

Glory speculated on what he was telling her. The

16

beautiful beach house she had stumbled into was obviously just a place for leisure, so Darcy must be quite wealthy. His partnership in a dignified-sounding law firm provided the same evidence. With that background it would be normal to expect him to be on the side of the rich and powerful, not the little man. Yet every indication was that Darcy was a crusader. Her original impression of him as a compassionate man had been correct.

"I was very fortunate to have found you," she commented soberly.

He made light of it. "I was the lucky one. How many damsels in distress turn out to be this beautiful?" He laughed. "I just hope the voters don't find out I spent the night with a gorgeous emerald-eyed redhead."

Glory's distress showed on her face. "That would be a problem for you, wouldn't it? Maybe I—"

"I was just joking, honey." He grinned mischievously. "Actually, I might get a lot of votes out of it. All the men would think I must be some kind of guy."

She attempted to match his light mood. Displaying her bare fingers, she remarked, "Well, at least neither of us is married."

When they reached the house, Darcy showed Glory to a spacious guest room overlooking the beach. It was furnished in soft tones of blue and beige to harmonize with the sea and sand on the other side of the large picture windows.

Everything was dark outside now, however, a muted landscape composed of blacks and grays that matched Glory's somber mood. She was staring at the foam-capped waves crashing against the shore when Darcy returned with something over his arm.

"This is the best I can do." He held out a navy silk pajama top, his gaze going over her slender figure. "I'm afraid you'll get lost in it."

"Thank you. It's . . . it will be just fine." She was

pleased that he didn't have any feminine apparel around.

Darcy hesitated for a moment, then his hand cupped her cheek, stroking it gently. "Get a good night's sleep, honey. Everything's going to look better in the morning."

After he had gone, Glory undressed and slipped into the unfamiliar bed. She stared up at the ceiling. What would happen if Darcy were wrong? Before the little demons of fear could brandish their pitchforks once more, Glory's eyelids started to droop. The medication the doctor had given her began to work.

She slept deeply for a couple of hours, then the nightmares started. There was a man in them, a blond man with cruel eyes and a twisted smile. He was chasing her. Glory ran through a tortuous maze, her breath coming in painful gasps as she tried to escape. Every turn led her deeper into the intricate puzzle as the blond man gained on her steadily, his easy lope like that of a predatory animal. Finally she saw daylight ahead, a way out of the labyrinth she was trapped in. As Glory raced toward safety, her lungs bursting with the effort, a hand fastened painfully on her shoulder. The man was dragging her inexorably back.

"No! No! I won't! You can't make me!" she screamed.

Strong arms curved around her, sparking a wild resistance. Her slim body twisted and arched, her small fists pounding to no avail. The man overcame her efforts easily.

Finally Darcy pinned both of her wrists in one of his big hands, shaking her with the other. "It's all right, honey. You're just having a bad dream. Wake up."

Glory looked at him in bewilderment, tears streaming down her pale cheeks. "Wha—what?"

"You were dreaming." He smoothed her tumbled hair, gently tucking a long strand behind her ear. "You're safe now. Nobody's going to hurt you."

She stared up at him with frightened eyes, details of the dream fading into a formless sense of horror. "Oh, Darcy, it was so awful."

Without thinking, she reached out for him, sliding her arms inside his pajama coat in an instinctive need for human contact.

He stiffened as her cheek nestled against the crisp, black hair on his chest. But when he would have drawn back, her arms tightened and her hands wandered restlessly over the suddenly tense muscles of his broad back.

"There was a man," she whispered. "That's all I remember . . . except that he was so evil."

Darcy's arms closed around her, holding her so tightly that she could hear the steady thump of his heart. His lips brushed her forehead. "Don't think about it, sweetheart."

His calmness was reassuring. Unconsciously Glory pressed closer, as if seeking to absorb some of his strength. She felt so safe in his arms. Gradually she became aware of his quickened breathing and of the fact that the curling hair on his chest was tickling her bare breasts.

Drawing back, she was horrified to see that her pajama top had come unbuttoned during her struggles. She had thrown herself practically nude into Darcy's arms!

For just an instant his eyes feasted on her small, rounded breasts, the rosy nipples looking like pink buds against her pearly skin. Then Darcy's long fingers swiftly fastened the buttons before she could make a move to do it.

"I—I'm so sorry," she murmured, warm color suffusing her pale cheeks. "I didn't know what I was doing."

"I knew that." His eyes glowed like topaz. "I wish it were otherwise." Getting up from the bed, he started for the door. "You'll be all right now. Go back to sleep."

She jumped out of bed. "Oh, no, I couldn't bear to have that same dream again."

He glanced at her long slim legs and bare thighs, looking away almost immediately. "I'll give you one of those tranquilizers the doctor prescribed. You're going to take it," he said firmly when she started to protest. "You need to sleep—and I need a cold shower," he muttered as he left the room.

Glory's fears proved groundless. The rest of her sleep was peaceful—unlike Darcy's. After tossing and turning for what remained of the night, he got up and dressed in a pair of brown cords and a matching cashmere sweater over an open-neck sport shirt.

Glory was sleeping peacefully when he looked in on her. He closed the door quietly and went into the kitchen to check the contents of the refrigerator. Outside of some beer and assorted cold cuts, there wasn't much. He hadn't intended to do any cooking.

Darcy stood in the middle of the room, reflecting. His guest would sleep for a couple of hours yet after the pill he'd given her. There was plenty of time to go to the market before she awakened. On an impulse, he decided to walk to the store instead of taking the car. Perhaps some exercise would get rid of the tension that was tying him up in knots.

The crisp morning air was bracing. His long legs covered the distance briskly until he rounded a bend in the road and saw the two police cars. They were parked beside a convertible that was lying on its side in a ditch.

Darcy knew one of the officers who was prowling around with a notebook in his hand. He was part of the small private police force that guarded the exclusive enclave that included Darcy's house. The officers were acquainted with most of the community and kept a special watch over the homes when their owners were absent.

"Hi, Pete," Darcy greeted the man. "That looks like a nasty one. Anybody hurt?"

"Hello, Mr. Lord. You're up early." He jerked his thumb toward the car. "I don't know. There was no one around when we got here."

"That's a good sign. Whoever it was walked away from it."

"Maybe. I think we're in for trouble anyway."

Darcy raised his eyebrows. "What's the problem?"

"The car is registered to Glory Wentworth," the officer said tersely.

"So?" The name was vaguely familiar, but Darcy couldn't place it.

"Glory Wentworth," Pete repeated significantly. "The girl who married Dudley Wentworth's son, Marshall."

Darcy made an involuntary grimace. "Now I remember."

"They had a place down here a while back. Sold it, though. The old man didn't come down much, and I guess it wasn't lively enough for young Mr. Wentworth." Pete's eyes met Darcy's in a meaningful glance.

Darcy knew what he was referring to. Marshall Wentworth used to give loud parties that went on most of the night. They always included a lot of beautiful young girls, and there was usually nude bathing. The neighbors were forbearing until Marshall and his guests thought it was fun to ring their doorbells in the middle of the night. Then the locals lodged a blizzard of complaints. The house was sold after some of them threatened to take their grievances to his father.

Darcy had never met Marshall, a fact he considered extremely good fortune. He knew all about him, though. The Wentworth rubber factory was one of the largest industries in Los Angeles, employing hundreds of people. Among other things, they made tires for planes and automobiles.

Like everyone else who could read, Darcy knew about Marshall's marriage three months previously. It was more than just a social event. Because of his father's prominence, it was treated as a news story by the press. The added Cinderella angle didn't hurt either.

Darcy remembered seeing Glory's picture in the paper, but it didn't do her justice. There was no way he would have recognized her from the grainy print. It couldn't capture the glowing vibrance of her flame red hair or the translucence of her flawless skin. In black and white the color of her emerald green eyes was lost. Even her exquisite features were reduced to mere candy box prettiness.

Darcy didn't read the details of this storybook romance in the papers, but he couldn't avoid hearing about it on the nightly news. If he wanted to find out the football scores, he had to sit through the recurring story of how a poor twenty-two-year-old girl whose father was a lowly foreman at the Wentworth factory met and married the handsome son of the owner.

Pete's voice recalled him to the present. "If Mrs. Wentworth was driving that car, I'd sure like to know where she is now. All hell is going to break loose if she's been injured and the police weren't there to help."

Darcy didn't know what kept him from revealing anything. "Maybe she wasn't in the car," he suggested casually.

"I hope you're right," Pete replied fervently. "But somebody was. What happened to them?"

"I'm sure you'll find out," Darcy told him.

His thoughts were somber on the way home. Everything he knew about Glory was diametrically opposed to the young woman who had come to his door last night. Darcy had automatically assumed that Wentworth's bride was one of the nubile playgirls who hung out at his parties—a little shrewder than most but basically a hard little opportunist. The facts surrounding her humble origins seemed to clinch the matter. Why else would a raving beauty like Glory marry a wimp like Marshall except for money?

Darcy was forced to accept that fact, although her whole demeanor denied it. Maybe Glory could have fooled him if she'd tried, but she was in no condition to be putting up a front last night. Remembering her painful embarrassment when her jacket had fallen open and he had glimpsed her beautiful body, Darcy couldn't see Glory frolicking nude with assorted men and women. There had to be another explanation. Maybe she wasn't Glory Wentworth after all. Even as the vain hope surfaced, he recognized it as futile.

Darcy's mouth twisted in self-mockery. You're just annoyed because the lady has reformed, he told himself. She has too much to lose to risk it on a one-night stand. Yet the memory of how she had clung to him made a pulse beat rapidly at his temple.

The house was still quiet when Darcy returned. He carried the groceries into the kitchen and unpacked the paper bags. After measuring coffee into the percolator, he put bacon in a frying pan, then made some orange juice with the electric juicer. All his movements were deliberate, as though he felt some kind of action were necessary.

"Good morning." Glory stood shyly in the doorway.

Darcy's face was expressionless. "Good morning. Did you sleep well—the rest of the night?"

"Yes, I . . . I didn't have any more bad dreams."

"That's good."

She looked at him uncertainly. "If you'll wait till I get dressed, I'll do that."

"That's all right. I'm quite capable of making breakfast," he answered evenly.

Glory hesitated in the doorway for a moment before vanishing.

After she had gone, Darcy groaned. What right did

he have to sit in judgment of her? She had her own reasons for doing what she had done. The fact that he found it totally insupportable was *his* problem. It was just that the thought of that exquisite girl selling herself to a man like Wentworth was intolerable. Darcy gritted his teeth as he told himself it was none of his business.

When Glory returned a short time later she was fully dressed and carried her jacket over her arm. The jade green blouse, which hugged her curves, matched the darkened color of her eyes.

"I want to thank you for everything," she said haltingly. "I'll be going now."

He looked at her impassively. "Where are you going?"

For a moment panic flared in her eyes, then she got it under control. "I don't know exactly, but I've imposed on you long enough."

He gave her a piercing stare. "You still don't remember?"

"No, I—no."

The hint of tears in her eyes penetrated his hostility. "Well, it's nothing to worry about. These things take time."

"You said I'd have my memory back by this morning," she reminded him.

"So I was off by a day or two." A wide grin showed his white teeth.

Glory's own smile was tentative. "You'll forgive me if I don't trust your predictions anymore."

"Have you ever trusted any man?" he demanded, his mood changing.

Her eyes widened. "I don't know."

A rush of emotions contorted Darcy's strong face. "Forget I ever said that." He propelled her into a chair at the round breakfast table. "What you need now is a good breakfast. Coffee is coming up, followed by freshly squeezed orange juice and bacon and eggs."

"It does smell awfully good," she admitted. "I don't think I've eaten in quite a while. It's just that I feel guilty about staying any longer."

"You're doing me a favor. There's nothing sadder than eating alone."

When Darcy placed a steaming plate in front of her, Glory discovered that she was starving. For a brief period they ate in a companionable silence. After the first pangs of hunger had been satisfied, she gave him a troubled look. "I want to apologize for last night."

Darcy reached for another piece of toast. "Anyone can have a bad dream. It was understandable under the circumstances."

"You know what I'm talking about." She bent her head over her plate, her long eyelashes feathering her flushed cheeks. "I don't usually act like that."

His firm mouth formed a straight line. "How do you know?"

Her eyes flew open, meeting his with indignation. "I may not remember my name, but I know I'm not the kind of woman who would throw herself at a man!"

"Unless there was something in it for you," he murmured, almost inaudibly.

"What?"

"It isn't important," he said. "You didn't throw yourself at me. Nothing happened, so it isn't worth talking about."

"It is to me," she insisted. The subtle change from last night's solicitude bothered her. Did he really think her behavior had been a come-on? Could he possibly imagine that she was faking this whole thing?

"Why do you care what I think?" Darcy demanded.

Glory felt as though a life preserver had been pried from her hands. She was back in a pit of darkness, alone in a hostile world. She put her napkin on the table, then rose to her feet. "I think I've overstayed my welcome.

25

Thank you for everything you've done for me. I'll be going now."

"Where, Glory?" he asked tersely.

"That isn't any concern of—" She stopped abruptly. "What did you say?"

"I called you Glory. Does that ring a bell?"

Shaking fingers covered her mouth. "Glory . . ."

He watched her closely. "Glory Wentworth. How about that?"

Her legs felt like cooked spaghetti. As they gave under her she slowly sank into the chair. "I know that name."

"It's your name, Glory. You're Mrs. Marshall Wentworth."

"No!" The agonized cry was wrenched out of her.

It was a curious reaction. "I thought you'd be pleased," Darcy said slowly.

"How did you find out?" she whispered.

"Your car was found this morning in a ditch not far from here. You must have taken that curve too fast. There was no sign of another vehicle's being involved."

"Who"—she had to stop to moisten her dry lips— "who found it?"

"The police. I stopped to talk to them when I went out for groceries this morning."

"Did you tell them I was here?"

"No." Darcy was glad she didn't ask why, since he couldn't explain his reasons to her anymore than he could to himself.

Her slight body relaxed its rigid pose until he reached for the phone. "What are you doing?" she asked sharply.

"I'm going to call your husband."

Her cold fingers covered his with surprising strength, forcing the receiver back into its cradle. "Don't do that."

"Why not? He's probably going out of his mind with

26

worry." Darcy's eyes narrowed appraisingly. "Do you *want* him to suffer?"

"No, of course not! I just want . . ." Glory clutched her temples, closing her eyes as though in unbearable pain. "I can't think! Oh, what am I going to do?" she moaned.

Darcy's big hands were warm on her slim shoulders. "It doesn't matter that you can't remember everything yet," he reassured her, moved by her anguish. "The main thing is that we know who you are. Everything else will come back to you in time."

She opened her eyes then, looking up at him with misery etched on her delicate flowerlike face. "That's the whole trouble. Everything *has* come back to me!"

CHAPTER TWO

"Would you like to tell me about it?" Darcy asked gently.

"No! Yes . . . I don't know." Glory looked at him hopelessly.

He took her hands and held them tightly. "The last thing I want to do is put pressure on you, honey. You've been through enough already. But I have a broad shoulder you can cry on if you feel the urge."

She shook her head. "You must be getting very tired of my doing that."

"Is that the impression I give?"

"Not last night. But this morning . . ." Her voice trailed off.

"I think I've been guilty of the gravest sin in the legal profession," he said somberly, "judging a case before hearing all the evidence."

She gazed at him uncertainly. "I don't understand."

"Never mind." He sat her down at the table, then seated himself across from her. "Tell me what's bothering you. Why don't you want me to call your husband?"

"I never want to see him again!"

"Don't you think you'd feel better if you told me about it?"

Indecision ravaged her delicate face. "It's such an ugly story. I don't know if I can talk about it."

He was silent for a moment. "You must have been very young when you met Wentworth," Darcy said unexpectedly.

Glory stared out at the ocean, which was calm this morning. The sun glinted off rippling blue water that gave no hint of last night's turbulence.

"I was twenty-one, fresh out of college, and wondering where I was going to get a job," she answered slowly. "I soon found out that the degree I was so proud of didn't mean a lot."

Darcy's face was expressionless. "How long did you look?"

"Not very long; I met Marshall."

Darcy looked at the pure line of her profile, the long slender length of her graceful neck. His mouth twisted slightly. "The higher the rewards, the greater the effort usually required. Perhaps you should have looked a little harder for a job."

She turned her head then, staring at Darcy as though seeing him for the first time. "You think I married Marshall for his money?"

Darcy shrugged. "It was merely an observation. You don't have to justify yourself to me."

"I wish that *had* been the reason," she answered bitterly. "It would have made a lot more sense than the real one."

Darcy was politely skeptical. "Your father was a foreman at the Wentworth factory, I believe."

"So naturally I would jump at the chance to marry the boss's son?" Glory's smile was sardonic. "Poor girl triumphs over humble beginnings. I see you've read the newspaper accounts."

Darcy made an impatient gesture. "It was the kind of story the media dotes on. Are you saying you were really in love with Wentworth?"

Glory sighed. "That's the worst of it—I had doubts from the very beginning."

"What resolved them?"

"I suppose Marshall did. Or maybe my family." She took a deep breath. "I met Marshall for the first time when I went to pick up my father at the factory one afternoon. Dad's car was in the shop and he expected to take the bus home. I had been to the beach that day, and when I got back and found out about it I volunteered to pick him up. I didn't want to get out of the car in shorts and a T-shirt, but since Dad didn't expect me, I was afraid I might miss him if I didn't wait at the gate."

"That's where Wentworth saw you and scraped up an acquaintance," Darcy interposed dryly.

He could just imagine how she had looked, with those long slim legs tanned from the sun and the T-shirt molding her firm breasts. The experience of holding that pliant body in his arms was still very much with Darcy. By the time Wentworth had gotten around to her beautiful face framed by that flaming silky hair, he would have been completely bowled over.

Glory shook her head. "Dad introduced us; it was all very proper. And Marshall was very polite when I apologized for the way I was dressed." She looked down at her clasped hands. "I could tell that he found me attractive, but he didn't come on strong or anything."

"He would hardly do that in front of your father," Darcy observed.

"I suppose so. Anyway, I was completely taken by surprise when he called that evening to ask me for a date."

"You must have been quite naive." Darcy smiled.

"The gossip writers would be very surprised to learn that I turned him down," she said ruefully. "Almost as surprised as Marshall was."

"He didn't take no for an answer, I gather?"

"It only made him more determined. I didn't know then that he'd do anything to get his own way." Her eyes were troubled. "I've always wondered if he would have lost interest if I'd been as eager to go out with him as all his other women were."

Darcy's gaze lingered on her captivating features. "Take it from another man: it wouldn't have made any difference."

Glory wasn't convinced, but she didn't pursue the subject. "He sent flowers—huge bouquets, sprays of orchids. He telephoned at all hours of the day and night. It got to be embarrassing."

"Did you actually dislike him at first?" Darcy asked curiously. "Is that why you refused all his invitations?"

"It wasn't that. I just didn't think it was a good idea to date the son of my father's boss."

"How did your parents feel about it?"

"They didn't agree." At the expression on Darcy's face, Glory added hurriedly, "They didn't try to urge me. They only said they didn't see anything wrong with it."

"I see." Darcy was carefully noncommittal.

After hesitating for a moment, Glory continued, "Finally it seemed easier to go out with him. I figured that would satisfy his pride. Not that it was a hardship," she explained. "I don't want to give that impression. Marshall is very attractive, and he can be extremely charming when he wants to be."

Darcy nodded. "He gave it his best effort?"

"Yes, he brought my mother candy, and he bought me silly little gifts—ten pounds of gumdrops, a furry little bear to put on my bed. I didn't realize till later that it was real mink. He took me to all the finest places, restaurants I'd only read about, and the best seats at the theater."

"Then he asked you to marry him?"

"Not right away." A pink flush colored Glory's high cheekbones.

Darcy got the picture. After wining and dining her, Wentworth made his move. When she turned him down —because that's obviously what must have happened— it would have come as a rude shock. A spoiled kid like that would have expected her to fall into his bed gratefully. Was that why he married her, because he couldn't get her any other way? The burning question remained, Why did Glory marry *him?*

"Marshall was very . . . I tried to break it off several times." Her embarrassment was obvious. "I'd dated a lot of men in college; they were boys actually, compared with Marshall. He was very experienced." Her flame-colored hair hid her flushed face as Glory bent her head. "I suppose it's almost laughable for a twenty-one-year-old woman to be a virgin nowadays."

So he had been right. "Not necessarily," Darcy said gently.

"I knew I was out of my depth, but he was extremely clever. The pressure he exerted was very subtle. No man had ever made such a concerted attack on my emotions. I was confused," she said honestly. "The side of himself that Marshall presented to me was exciting, glamorous, and persuasive. My parents were delighted, and my friends all told me how lucky I was. When I still wavered, he took me to meet his family."

"What kind of reception did you get?"

"Mixed." She acknowledged the question with a slight smile. "Marshall's father was quite pleasant, but my future mother-in-law was distinctly cool." Glory laughed, her first relaxed emotion of the day. "It didn't bother me, though, because I've always heard that no girl is ever acceptable to the mother of a son."

"So I've heard," Darcy agreed with a grin.

"The one I made a real hit with was Marshall's grandmother. She's the grande dame of the clan; everyone defers to her. Perhaps because she holds the controlling stock in the family business," Glory added dryly. "Once she put her stamp of approval on me, everyone else made sure to follow suit. One thing I'll say about old Mrs. Wentworth: she's no snob. I think the fact that I worked my way through college was actually a plus in her eyes." A saddened look crossed Glory's face. "This is going to hurt her."

Darcy made note of the fact that Glory's only regrets were for Wentworth's grandmother. "She sounds like a very strong old lady. I presume that after she added her persuasion, it was all over but the wedding."

Glory nodded. "After she gave her blessing, Marshall intensified his courtship. Among other things, he got my father a raise. Oh, he didn't take credit for it, but there was no doubt about his being responsible. The only thing he wouldn't do was help me get a job. I wanted to work for a year before we got married, just to experience a little independence. But the only jobs I could get were so menial that I couldn't even have supported myself. And Marshall wouldn't help me get anything better."

"He's smarter than I thought," Darcy murmured, almost inaudibly.

"Then while I was vacillating, his grandmother became ill. It wasn't anything life threatening. We both knew that, but she pulled out all the stops. She told me how much it would mean to her to see her only grandchild married and settled down." Glory shrugged. "By that time I had accepted the fact that I was going to marry Marshall, so there didn't seem to be any reason to wait."

Darcy smiled sardonically. "And the old lady made a miraculous recovery in time for the big shindig."

"I wanted a small ceremony," Glory said, anger in her voice. "The bride's family is supposed to pay for the wedding, and it was all we could have afforded anyway. But that didn't suit my mother-in-law. Once it was an unavoidable fact, she took over." Glory ran weary fingers through her long hair. "Nero could have used her to stage one of his more memorable orgies. But I'm sure you know all about that. The twelve bridesmaids—none

33

of whom were friends of mine, the orchids flown in from Hawaii, the crystal bowls filled with caviar."

Darcy watched her face. "And the grand honeymoon in Europe?"

"Yes." She became even more pale, if possible.

Darcy was flooded by impotent fury. Wentworth had wreaked his vengeance for being thwarted so long. He hadn't bothered to be gentle or considerate once the prize was in his hands.

With an effort Darcy kept the anger out of his voice. "All of that was three months ago?"

She looked faintly incredulous. "It seems like an eternity."

"Then you came back to Los Angeles and settled down?" he prompted.

"If you can call it that. I didn't realize that Marshall needed to be on the go every instant. If there wasn't a party at someone else's house, we had to have one at ours. He was like an insecure little boy—afraid he was missing something." She looked away. "Or maybe he was just bored being alone with me."

"That isn't even worth refuting," Darcy told her.

Glory was too preoccupied to take note of his tribute. "Marshall's grandmother gave us a house in Beverly Hills for a wedding present. His mother hired a decorator. When we got back from our honeymoon the place was completely furnished, down to the last vase and ornament. I guess she didn't trust me to do it myself. She was probably right. I wouldn't have known how to hire our servants either."

"So essentially, you had nothing to do," Darcy said gently.

"I wasn't even as useful as one of those Dresden figurines!" She sprang up to pace the floor restlessly, her arms wrapped around her trembling body. "I can't imagine why Marshall married me."

Darcy thought he knew. Glory was strikingly beautiful. She would command attention wherever she went and reflect glory on the man who had won such a prize. From everything he was learning about Wentworth, Darcy knew him to be a man who needed admiration—even if it came to him secondhand. Of course, there was another more obvious reason why he married her. Darcy tried to find a delicate way of putting it.

"Sometimes a man doesn't want his wife distracted by household problems," he said tactfully, "especially when they're first married."

She gave a short mirthless laugh. "He didn't even need me for that. Marshall has always enjoyed the attention of women. I know now that it was foolish to expect a small piece of paper to change all that."

"I see," Darcy answered quietly.

She raised her trembling chin high. "So did everyone else. I couldn't bear their pity, but I didn't know what to do about it. How could I leave my husband after a little over a month?"

Darcy frowned. "Do you mean that almost from the beginning . . ."

She nodded. "Finally I couldn't stand it anymore, and I went home to my parents. Fortunately I left my bags in the car while I went in to prepare them. They were very happy to see me and wanted to know all about my glamorous new life. Before I got around to telling them, Dad started to talk about the factory. He said he had been forced to lay off some of the men under him. Mother said that she felt sorry for their families but that she couldn't help being grateful that Dad's job was secure because of his son-in-law."

A muscle jerked at the point of Darcy's rigid jaw. "So you didn't tell them?"

"How could I?"

"Very easily. If you can't turn to your parents for help, there's something mighty wrong."

"They weren't to blame; they had no idea. I didn't

even know if I was doing the right thing. I had to consider that maybe it was partly my fault." She ignored Darcy's low growl of protest. "Besides, I felt like such a failure."

"Didn't you ever confront him with any of this?" Darcy demanded.

"Oh, yes." A faint smile lightened Glory's strained expression. "I have quite a temper to go with this red hair, and I've never been a doormat."

"But you let Wentworth talk you around," Darcy stated disgustedly.

"He didn't even try," she replied simply. "Marshall merely said I didn't have any proof that would stand up in court. He said that if I left him after such a short time, it would confirm everyone's suspicion that I had married him for his money. He said my engagement and wedding rings alone cost more than most people made in a year." Noticing Darcy's automatic glance at her bare fingers, she added, "I threw them in his face before I left."

"Good for you!"

"It was the only satisfaction I had. Marshall couldn't understand why I couldn't . . . 'hang loose' was the way he put it, I believe. Not that he expected me to adopt his moral code. The strange thing was that he turned very ugly if a man paid too much attention to me —even one of his friends. That's what finally brought things to a head."

"I'm glad something did," Darcy muttered.

"It was at a party last Friday night. Someone had brought a guest from out of town, a really stunning divorcée. I could recognize all the signs when Marshall got his first glimpse of her." Glory's soft mouth twisted in a grimace of distaste. "In the beginning, it used to hurt terribly, but by now I was like a spectator being forced to sit through a disagreeable movie again. I left him to make all his opening gambits and went to dance with Sloan Shelton. Sloan is everything Marshall would like to be," Glory remarked thoughtfully. "He's a top athlete, he makes friends easily, and everyone admires him—a thoroughly nice, laid-back person. He thought I might be upset watching Marshall's antics, so he took me for a walk around the grounds."

"I should think that would suit Wentworth perfectly."

Glory shook her head. "I told you, Marshall was very possessive. He'd also had a few drinks. When we came back to the house, he accused Sloan of making a play for me. He said he was going to fix him so that he was in no condition to make a pass at anyone. Sloan was less than amused. When Marshall swung on him Sloan decked him with one punch."

Darcy smiled grimly. "I wish I'd been there."

"Count your blessings," Glory said tersely. "It was a really nasty scene, but nothing like the one we had when we got home. Marshall accused me of everything under the sun, and I blew sky-high. I told him that this time I was leaving, and I didn't care what stories he spread. I don't know if he believed me or not. When I left he was still agonizing over the debacle at the party."

Darcy could understand how the loss of his dignity would affect Wentworth. An insecure man to begin with, he had made himself look ridiculous, something he couldn't handle. He would have to find a way to shift the responsibility onto someone else. It was with a sense of foreboding that Darcy waited for the conclusion of Glory's story.

"I didn't want to put this burden on my parents, so I flew to San Francisco to see my sister," she continued. "Carole is five years older than me, and I've always looked up to her." Glory's generous mouth curved as she smiled for the first time since she'd met Darcy. "She's so calm and analytical. After letting me cry on her shoulder and get it all out of my system, she dissected the problem like a mathematical equation. While acknowledging that Marshall was spoiled rotten, she pointed out that he must really love me. I was the one he had married out of innumerable choices. But after being a bachelor for thirty-one years, he was probably finding it as difficult as I was to adjust to married life."

Darcy snorted inelegantly. "You bought that garbage?"

"I wanted to believe she was right," Glory explained patiently. "It's a terrible thing to think you've messed up your life when you're only twenty-two."

"You're right, of course." Darcy squeezed her hand contritely.

"I started remembering all the good times Marshall and I had together before we were married, and how fond I had been of him. In the normal, loving atmosphere of my sister's house, I began to have hope. If Marshall and I could just sit down and talk about our problems, surely we could work everything out."

"So you went back?"

Glory was too intent to see Darcy's disgusted expression. "I was so charged up after talking to Carole that I couldn't wait to get home. She has three little children, so it was Saturday night before we found time for an undisturbed conversation. And then we talked for hours. It was ten o'clock before we finished, but I knew I would never sleep. I decided to take a plane that night. I could be home by midnight."

"You didn't let Wentworth know?"

"There wasn't time. I took a taxi from the airport. Marshall was in bed when I got home—he looked as though he'd been there ever since I left. He had a two-day growth of beard and the room was a mess. There were dirty dishes on the dresser and an empty Scotch bottle on the floor. The one on the nightstand had only a small amount left in it." Glory's face reflected the distaste she'd felt. "At first I was full of remorse. I had

38

driven him to this. I told him I was sorry for everything, that we'd start over and our marriage would be better."

"*You* apologized to *him?*"

"I thought he was suffering because of me," she explained. "Then he said he knew I'd come crawling back, that I wasn't about to give up all the luxury I'd never had before. He called me disgusting names. When I realized how wrong I'd been we had a terrible argument. I told him I was leaving for good this time, that all I wanted from him was my freedom." Glory's eyes were a feverish green in her pale face as she reached the climax of her story. "Marshall grabbed me and threw me on the bed. He said he'd never let me go, that I belonged to him—he'd bought and paid for me. He started to . . . He tried to make me . . ." Her head drooped like a flower on a slender stalk.

Darcy got up abruptly, thrusting his clenched fists in his pockets. His face was rigid as he pictured the brutal assault that was no better than attempted rape.

"I managed to get away from him and run to the door." Her voice was very faint now. "Marshall came after me like a maniac, but he tripped over the suitcase I'd left in the middle of the floor. It gave me a chance to escape. I rushed out of the house and got in my car. I didn't know where I was going; I just drove as fast as I could go."

Darcy stared at her intently. "Wentworth once had a house down here. Is that why you came to Malibu? Did you used to go there?"

Glory shook her head. "That was before I met him. I guess I headed down to the beach because there wasn't as much traffic and I could be alone."

"Do you remember the accident?"

She frowned in concentration. "Not really. The next thing I remember is walking along the beach and wondering what I was doing there."

"You must have taken that curve at a terrific rate of speed!" Darcy exclaimed.

"Do you think I was trying to commit suicide?" she asked somberly.

"Of course not!" He hunched down in front of her, then took her cold hands in his big warm ones. "You've had an experience that would devastate a person with a lot more experience, but from what you've told me, you're a fighter. You have too much going for you to let this ruin your life."

"I hope you're right," she said sighing.

"I know I am."

There was deep gratitude in her voice. "It was good of you to listen to me. I'm okay now."

"You'll feel even better once we get you disentangled from that little sadist," Darcy assured her. "As soon as you pull yourself together, we'll go and collect your things."

"No!" When he looked at her in surprise, she explained, "Everything in that house was bought with Marshall's money. I don't want anything from him."

"That's the spirit!" Darcy said with satisfaction. "You needn't worry, honey. I'll take care of you."

"Please don't take this the wrong way, Darcy, but I don't want anything from you either," she said carefully. "For once in my life I'm going to stand on my own two feet. Whatever happens from now on will be strictly my responsibility."

"That's very admirable, but you'll need a place to live and some money until you get a job."

"I have a small bank account in my maiden name." Glory's long eyelashes fell. "I didn't tell Marshall about it because he would have laughed at me. It's not very much, but I wanted it to buy him birthday presents and things out of my own money."

Darcy tipped her chin up with a long forefinger as he

looked down at her tenderly. "Has anyone ever told you that you're a very nice human being?"

She managed a smile. "Not in a long time."

"Then let me be the first to say it."

Suddenly something electric charged the air. A glow lighted Darcy's golden brown eyes, turning them luminous. His arms circled her narrow waist, drawing her closer as his dark head bent slowly toward her bright one. Glory caught her breath, seeing him as a man for the first time instead of a vague someone who had given her shelter. A tiny ripple started at the base of her spine and traveled throughout her midsection. The unexpectedness of it startled her. She held him off with her palms against his shoulders, feeling the shifting muscles under his smooth skin.

As soon as Darcy saw the uncertainty in her eyes he released her. He got to his feet, his lithe body moving with fluid grace. "Well, how about it?" he asked casually. "Shall we go apartment hunting?"

"I . . . Yes, that's a good idea."

The brief moment that had flared between them might never have been, leaving Glory with mixed emotions. Part of her had actually wanted him to kiss her. Wasn't that ridiculous? As though she didn't have enough trouble already! That crack on the head must have been more severe than she knew.

Glory stole a look at him from under her long eyelashes. Darcy had retrieved the Sunday paper from the front porch and was looking through the classified section. His profile was turned to her, clean-cut with a firm chin ending in a square jaw. He looked lean and fit and devastatingly handsome. No wonder he had released her as soon as she showed the slightest hesitancy. This man wouldn't have to force himself on any woman.

Then she thought of Marshall. He had always wanted to be tall and broad shouldered like Darcy. If Marshall had been four inches taller, would it have changed his personality? She doubted it. That streak of refined cruelty was in his genes. Remembering his lovemaking, Glory shuddered.

Darcy looked up from the newspaper. "There are a lot of apartments. I think the first thing you have to decide is where you want to live."

She looked at him helplessly. "I suppose it would make sense to live near work, but I don't know yet where I'm going to get a job."

"Let's take one thing at a time," he said, smiling. "How about the Wilshire district? It's halfway between downtown and the beach, and there's good transportation."

"That sounds practical," she agreed.

"Sunday is a good day to go looking, too," he told her. "Everyplace will be open."

Together they marked off likely prospects. Glory's spirits began to soar. The horrendous rents would eat up her small capital in nothing flat, she had neither a job nor any prospects of one, and she faced all the problems of a divorce. But she was free. *Free!*

Her green eyes sparkled. "Ready when you are, D. L."

His mobile mouth turned up at the corners. "Is this the same little waif who turned up on my doorstep last night?"

"Definitely not! You'll be glad to know that you're about to be relieved of your burden."

His hand smoothed her shining hair. "I never considered you that for a minute."

Glory felt herself melting inside. It wasn't just his kindness. Darcy exerted a powerful magnetism that was hard to resist, especially since he seemed to be drawn to her, too. But Glory knew it was something she wasn't entitled to—not as long as she was tied to Marshall.

She moved away reluctantly. "I guess we'd better get started."

* * *

They looked at so many apartments that Glory's head was swimming—and her euphoria of the morning had vanished. For the most part they were sterile little boxes, the furnishings suitable for a doctor's waiting room. None of which affected the price. The rents being asked were astronomical.

Darcy took note of her woebegone face. Squeezing her clenched fingers, he said comfortingly, "Don't worry, honey. We've only begun to fight."

She tried to muster a smile. "I feel like I've been knocked out in the first round."

"I know better than that. You're no quitter."

They were on their way to the next place on their list when they passed a gracious old house with a U-Haul truck out front. Several young people were loading it with odd pieces of furnishings. Darcy screeched to a halt at the curb.

"There doesn't happen to be a vacant apartment in that house, does there?" he asked a young woman in a jogging suit.

Her short curls bounced as she nodded her head. "It won't last long, though. It's the most fantastic place—I really hate to leave it."

A lanky young man joined them and put his arm around her shoulders. "We'll find something just as great in Texas, Franny. I'm being transferred," he explained.

"Talk to Mrs. Belmont if you're interested," she told Darcy. After eyeing the silver Mercedes parked at the curb, she added dubiously, "Although, I don't know if it will be fancy enough for you and your wife."

"I'm sure it will be." Glory put her arm around Darcy's waist, smiling up at him impishly. "Appearances are deceiving, aren't they, darling?"

The apartment was indeed the answer to all her prayers. It was both spacious and airy. The high ceilings

43

were festooned with elaborate scrollwork, and tall windows looked out on a glorious garden complete with a sundial and birdbath.

The furnishings were worn, but they had been good quality and still conveyed an aura of elegance. The sofa in the living room was plum-colored damask, its slightly frayed arms covered with hand-crocheted doilies. A petit point chair had a matching footstool, and there were two marble-topped Victorian tables.

The bedroom was furnished with a four-poster bed and a flounced dressing table. Both were covered in a matching floral print that was old-fashioned but charming. Tieback ruffled curtains at the windows were the finishing touch.

Glory threw her arms around Darcy's neck. "Isn't it heavenly? Oh, if only I can afford it!"

His arms closed automatically around her, holding Glory against him. "We'll figure it out," he said in a husky voice.

As she looked up into his darkly handsome face Glory caught her breath. And when he bent his head, her lips parted automatically, hoping for the touch of that firm mouth against her own.

"Did you want something?"

The high, reedy voice made Glory jump guiltily. Pulling out of Darcy's embrace, she turned to see a tiny, birdlike woman with gray hair arranged in an elaborate chignon at the back of her head. Her clothes seemed to be a mixture of the nineteenth and twentieth centuries. A fine old cameo brooch was fastened at the neck of an exquisite lace blouse that was tucked into a pair of lime green polyester slacks. Although her clothing was rather eccentric, the woman's bright little eyes looked exceedingly shrewd.

"Are—are you Mrs. Belmont?" Glory struggled for composure. When the woman nodded, she said breathlessly, "I'd love to rent this apartment—if it isn't too much money, that is."

"Not so fast, missy. I'll have to know something about you first. Who are you, to begin with?"

Glory's heart sank. Would she recognize her name from the newspapers? And would it work for or against her? She took a deep breath. "I . . . My name is Glory Prescott." It wasn't really a lie. She intended to resume her maiden name after the divorce.

"Are you Mr. Prescott?" the little old lady demanded of Darcy.

"No, I'm just a friend. Darcy Lord." He gave her his most charming smile. "The apartment is for . . . Ms. Prescott . . . only."

"I know you!" she exclaimed. "You're the one who gave it to that big automobile company, aren't you? Got what was coming to that poor woman with all those children. Didn't I read that you're going to run for the state senate?" Without waiting for an answer, she said, "You must tell me all about it. Come up to my place and I'll make a nice pot of tea."

"Wait!" Glory cried as the old lady was hustling Darcy out the door.

"You can come, too, my dear," Mrs. Belmont said over her shoulder.

"What about the apartment?"

"It's yours. Any friend of Mr. Lord's must be the right sort."

"But we haven't discussed the rent. I don't know if I can afford it."

"Oh, I'm sure we can work something out. Come along now; it's teatime."

Darcy laughed at Glory's dazed face. "I think you've found a home."

Over tea in the landlady's apartment, which was crammed with antiques, faded photographs, and mementos that covered every available surface, they found

45

out more about Mrs. Belmont. She was a childless widow who had evidently been left quite well off. After her husband died, she was reluctant to sell the big house that held so many happy memories for her, but it became lonely after a while. That's when she decided to divide the bottom floor into two apartments.

"I rent only to young people," she told them. "I love to hear their laughter. They've become my extended family—dozens of them over the years."

"You have no family of your own?" Darcy asked gently.

"Not a chick, not a child," Mrs. Belmont answered cheerfully. "You mustn't feel sorry for me, though. You know that old saying, You can pick your friends, but you're stuck with your family."

Darcy surveyed her pert, lined little face with a smile. "It would never occur to me to feel sorry for you."

The elderly lady returned his gaze with one of frank admiration. "I hope you're going to be coming around here often."

Darcy grinned. "You can count on it."

Glory felt like a leaf being carried over a waterfall. "About the rent, Mrs. Belmont . . ." she began desperately.

Glory had been honest about her situation, but it didn't seem to trouble the woman. "Why don't we just wait until you get a job? Then we'll see how much you can afford."

"But you can't—"

"I've been thinking about that, Glory." Darcy looked thoughtful. "I'm going to need someone to coordinate the workers at my campaign headquarters. How would you like the job?"

"I don't have any experience in politics," she answered reluctantly.

He shrugged. "Neither do I. We'll learn together."

"I can't let you do that, Darcy. I know why you're

46

making the offer. I'm grateful to you, but I'm not a charity case," she stated firmly.

He raised one eyebrow. "What makes you think I consider you one? If you come to work for me, you'll work harder than you ever have in your life." He gave her a slow smile that made her heart skip a beat. "After hours I can't promise what my conduct will be, but in the office, it will be strictly business. You'll earn every penny of your salary."

Glory hesitated. "I just feel you need someone with more experience."

Mrs. Belmont was watching their exchange with interest. "Of course if you don't feel you can handle the position, you're quite right in refusing, my dear," she murmured. "I can certainly understand your concern. We sheltered ladies aren't equipped to deal with the sort of people one is apt to meet."

Glory's green eyes sparkled angrily. "I didn't say I *couldn't* do it. I just felt it wouldn't be fair to Darcy."

"He doesn't look like the sort of man one imposes upon," Mrs. Belmont observed.

"Then it's all settled." Darcy and the old lady exchanged the merest glance.

"Delightful! When would you like to move in?" her landlady asked Glory.

"I thought . . . Could I have the apartment right now?"

"Certainly. I'll give you a key and you can start bringing your things over this evening."

Glory caught her lower lip between her small white teeth. "Well, I—that is, I don't really have—"

"Why don't I take you two lovely ladies out for dinner?" Darcy cut in smoothly. "Glory will have plenty of time to get settled later tonight."

Mrs. Belmont's shrewd eyes rested for a long moment on Glory's troubled face before turning to Darcy. "It's been a long time since I've had an invitation like that from such a charming gentleman, but I'm afraid I must decline. Ellen is coming to dinner. Ellen Dressler, the young woman who has the other apartment," she explained. Mrs. Belmont tipped her head to one side in a birdlike motion. "I think I hear her now. How nice; you can all get acquainted."

As she went to the door, Glory turned to Darcy with suppressed excitement. "I can scarcely believe it. In just one day, I have a new home, a new job, a new life!"

He took both of her hands and looked deeply into her eyes. "You deserve it, honey."

He was so close that she could smell the clean, masculine scent of his after-shave. It was like a mild aphrodisiac, making her feel warm and languorous. "I owe it all to you, Darcy. What would I have done without you?"

"You would have managed, but I'm glad I was there." His voice was husky.

A delicate cough announced Mrs. Belmont's return. Standing in the doorway with her was a slender young woman in her late twenties. She had short, glossy black hair, brown eyes, and a wide, generous mouth that was turned down now in a contemptuous twist as she regarded the couple on the couch.

Glory was puzzled by the scarcely veiled animosity being aimed their way.

"Ellen is a buyer at Bryman's Department Store," Mrs. Belmont announced brightly after the introduction had been made. "She's responsible for all the children's wear."

"That must be fun, getting to pick and choose," Glory commented. "I'm tempted to buy every adorable little ruffly thing I see, and I don't even have children."

"It's always the childless ones who rhapsodize over the little darlings," Ellen answered derisively.

"It sounds as though you don't care very much for

children, Ms. Dressler." Darcy's voice was carefully expressionless.

She shrugged. "They're all right, I guess. It's everything that goes with them."

"You mean diapers and bottles and things?" Glory asked. "I understand that phase is over with fast."

Darcy's eyes met Ellen's in a silent duel. "I don't think that's what Ms. Dressler had in mind."

Mrs. Belmont moved swiftly to dispel the suddenly charged atmosphere. "You and Ellen will have plenty of time to get acquainted," she told Glory. "Why don't you run along and start getting settled?"

"Yes, I'm certain Mr. Lord has plans for this evening," Ellen drawled with thinly concealed malice.

"You're right, Ms. Dressler—as I'm sure you *always* are," Darcy returned mockingly.

Before any more barbs could be exchanged, Mrs. Belmont shepherded them deftly out the door.

CHAPTER THREE

When they were in Darcy's car Glory turned to him with a slight frown. "Am I wrong, or did you get the feeling that that Dressler woman was being definitely hostile?"

"You weren't wrong."

"Why on earth would she act that way before even getting to know us?"

Darcy hesitated a moment, then shrugged. "Don't worry about it. You have your own problems."

Glory gave him a radiant smile. "Not anymore! Everything's coming up roses. Isn't Mrs. Belmont a darling? At first, I thought she was rather weird—that strange outfit and the casual way she rented me the apartment without even discussing money. But now I can see that she's just a little . . . well . . . unconventional, I guess you could say."

Darcy smiled appreciatively. "Don't be fooled by small eccentricities. That little old lady is extremely shrewd."

"She can't possibly know what she's done for me." Glory hugged herself rapturously. "I feel as though someone opened the door of my cage."

"In that case, how about some bird seed?" Darcy teased. "It's a little early, but I did promise you dinner."

Glory looked down at her rather rumpled clothing. "I feel too grubby to go anywhere. I've been in these same clothes since yesterday."

Darcy's eyes held a glow as they took in her lovely face and slender body. "You look better than most women after they've slaved over themselves for hours. However, it does bring up a point. That outfit represents your total wardrobe at the moment; you're going to need some clothes." He looked at his watch. "We can just make it if we hurry."

"Make what? Hurry where?"

"The shopping centers don't close until five thirty, so we have half an hour to do some intensive shopping." He gave her a wide grin. "You'll have to make some lightning-fast decisions."

Darcy drove to one of the better department stores where Glory was faced with the daunting task of selecting a complete wardrobe without trying anything on.

"You can exchange anything that doesn't fit," Darcy assured her. "Just buy some of everything. To save time, I'll take care of the lingerie department."

"No, wait! You can't—" But her protests were directed at his retreating back. "You don't even know my size," she called desperately.

He turned then, his eyes traveling comprehensively over her contours as his mouth curved in a sensuous smile. "I have a very retentive memory."

Glory's cheeks bloomed bright scarlet as she remembered that inadvertent moment in his arms. It made her even more reluctant to have him select her undergarments, but he was gone before she could argue about it.

By the time the store closed, Glory had loaded her own arms and those of several happy clerks. After Darcy had added his own purchases, the backseat of the sporty coupé was piled high.

"I have just fulfilled every woman's fantasy," she announced. "Buying everything in sight without once looking at a price tag."

"I thought you were very frugal. I didn't see one evening gown or fur coat."

The sparkle left her face. "I won't have any use for them."

Darcy cupped her chin in his hand, lifting it gently so she had to look at him. "Hey, there's a whole world out there. You have a lot of living still to do, Ms. Prescott."

Glory caught her breath at the use of her maiden name. "That's something I'd like to talk to you about, Darcy. Naturally, I wouldn't expect you to be my attorney, but perhaps you can give me some advice about who to go to for a divorce."

"We'll talk about it over dinner," he said, turning on the ignition key.

She hesitated. "I'd really like to shower and change first."

"I have an alternate suggestion. How about coming up to my apartment? I'll cook dinner while you get cleaned up."

"I don't think that would be a very good idea," Glory said carefully.

He gave her a penetrating look. "You mean you don't trust me?"

"That isn't it at all!" After everything he had done for her, Glory felt it was important to explain herself. "I was thinking about you. Politicians have to be very discreet. Under the circumstances I don't think it's a good idea for you to get involved with me."

"I wasn't aware that cooking dinner was getting 'involved.' However, I'll be happy to change my thinking," he teased.

"You know what I mean," she muttered.

His hand closed firmly over hers. "Listen to me, Glory. I'm running for the state senate because I think I'm qualified and I'd like to do some good. That doesn't mean I expect to give up my whole life to the job. If you're tired of my company, that's a valid reason for refusing my invitation. I won't accept any other."

Darcy's firm statement didn't allow any argument—

which pleased Glory greatly. She didn't really want to give him any.

His apartment was a penthouse atop one of the tall buildings lining Wilshire Boulevard in Westwood. All of Los Angeles was spread out from the terrace surrounding it—the Hollywood hills to the north, the ocean to the west, and the lights of the city in the other two directions. It was like viewing an animated painting. Red and green signals flashed on and off, toy cars darted in and out like lightning bugs, and jet liners overhead acted as mobiles.

The apartment was furnished in tranquil beiges and browns, in order not to distract from the splendors visible through the floor-to-ceiling glass windows. But when Glory tore her fascinated gaze away from the magnificent view, she noticed rare and costly ornaments placed unobtrusively around the spacious rooms. The furnishings were a mixture of antique and modern, blending into a comfortable, inviting atmosphere.

The difference from her own rigidly decorated home, where everything had to be of the same period, was like the contrast between diamonds and rhinestones. "Darcy, it's fantastic!" she exclaimed. "I could die happy here!"

He came very close, linking his hand around the back of her neck underneath the shining hair. "I'd rather you'd live happily," he murmured in a throaty voice.

Glory was suddenly acutely aware of this tall, lean man, as she had been aware of no other—certainly not Marshall. She had dated extensively in high school and college, having the usual crushes, but never had her emotions been engaged to this extent. With Darcy she felt all woman, wanting the things from him that a woman wanted from a man.

Glory took a quick breath, denying the treacherous demands of her body. She was still married. Until that could be remedied, she had no right to feel this way.

She moved gracefully aside, picking up a couple of her packages. "Would you mind if I showered now? I'll help with dinner as soon as I'm cleaned up."

Darcy didn't try to stop her; he seemed to understand. Lightening the situation with ease, he declared, "Nobody is allowed in my kitchen. Just tell me what you want to drink, and I'll leave it outside the bathroom door."

After her shower Glory donned a new pair of jeans and a pale blue oxford cloth shirt. She brushed her long hair until it crackled like the flames it resembled, then touched up her mouth with a slick of lip gloss.

When she appeared in the kitchen a few moments later, Darcy's unguarded appraisal was wholly masculine. His golden brown eyes flared briefly as they ranged over the narrow jeans that hugged her slim hips and rounded bottom, traveling upward to the close-fitting shirt that strained across her breasts.

He deliberately turned back to the stove. "That was good timing; dinner's ready."

Glory's voice was filled with compunction. "I'm sorry it took me so long. I really did mean to help."

"It's not too late." He handed her a package of matches. "You can light the candles. I've set the table by the window in the living room."

She accepted the matches, still feeling guilty. "I'll redeem myself by doing all the cleaning up after," she promised.

"That won't be necessary. I have a very competent lady who comes in every morning."

"I'm sure she wouldn't appreciate being greeted by a mess."

Darcy chuckled. "Through the years, Mrs. Bates has become remarkably tolerant. Nothing shocks her."

Glory gave him a covert look. What exactly did that mean? The various answers that occurred to her made her decide not to pursue the subject.

The tall, flickering candles cast a soft glow over the square rosewood table, illuminating without distracting from the magnificent view outside. Lights had come on all over the city, decking it in multicolored jewels. From this height the stars seemed almost within reach, their steady light a calm contrast to the darting flashes below. Glory could scarcely tear her eyes away from the enchanting sight.

Darcy pretended displeasure. "After I slaved over a hot stove, the least you could do is show a little interest in the magnificent meal I cooked."

She turned dazzled eyes to him. "I can eat any old time. I'd much rather drink in this glorious view."

"It isn't your last chance," he answered dryly. "I had already planned on asking you back."

After a brief look at his handsome face, Glory directed her attention at her plate. "You needn't feel responsible for me, Darcy. I've imposed on you far too much as it is."

"I don't remember complaining—and you didn't impose."

"How can you say that after I ruined your whole weekend? I know you intended using that time to work. Instead of that, I kept you up all night and used up your entire Sunday."

"I'll admit you kept me up all night, but that wasn't entirely your fault—at least not intentionally." The smile on his face was rueful. "I enjoyed today, though. It was a lot more rewarding than working."

"But not as productive."

"I work best under pressure, anyway," Darcy said dismissively. He glanced at her plate and saw that she had scarcely touched it. "Eat your dinner. How can I fatten you up if you don't cooperate? We'll have to do something about your appetite," he scolded.

Glory picked up her fork obediently, although she wasn't really hungry. The events of the last two days, plus the company of the intensely masculine man across the table, were acting like a nervous stimulant. Her appetite was suppressed under the keen awareness of all her other senses.

She made a conscious effort to relax. "You evidently haven't heard that a woman can never be too rich or too thin."

Darcy's level appraisal noted the petal soft skin stretched too tightly across the high cheekbones, the hollow at the base of her graceful neck. "I have a feeling one of your conditions was caused by the other."

Glory's lashes fell as memories came flooding back. Her fingers clenched unconsciously around a roll.

Darcy's big hand covered hers immediately. "I'm sorry, Glory. Forget I said that."

"It's all right. I can't exactly sweep my marriage under the rug, even if it did only last three months."

"I won't tell you to put it out of your mind because that would be stupid," he said gently. "I can assure you, however, that time will blur the edges." His hand tightened on hers. "Now, finish your dinner. You're going to need a lot of stamina to work for me."

She looked up at that. "Are you sure it's a good idea, Darcy? If I thought—"

"I'm sure," he interrupted firmly. "Have some more wine."

Glory finally managed to relax, helped along by several glasses of wine. By the time dinner was over she felt pleasantly languid. Darcy carried their coffee to the low table in front of the couch.

Glory sank down on the cushions with a little sigh of pleasure. The soft background music was soothing, and the view was spectacular.

"This is lovely, Darcy. But next time I come—if you really mean it about asking me—I won't be so useless."

Tiny embers turned his golden brown eyes molten, although his voice was carefully playful. "How can you call yourself useless? Haven't you ever heard that beauty is its own reward?"

A smile curved her generous mouth. "Thanks for the compliment, but you have your quotations mixed. It's virtue that is its own reward."

"I like my version better." The husky quality in his voice made a slight shiver travel down Glory's spine, although he made no move to touch her.

Turning her head, she pointed at a distant bright light. "What would that be?"

"That's the golden statue on top of the Mormon church," he informed her, accepting the change of subject. "And over there is Dodger Stadium. See all the klieg lights?"

The tenuous moment of intimacy passed. Under cover of their casual conversation, Glory examined her feelings. Perhaps she should feel guilty about having dinner alone with this man, but she didn't. Her marriage was over except for the legal machinery that would affirm what she already knew. Actually, it had been over as soon as Marshall satisfied his need to triumph.

Glory knew she wasn't rationalizing. She acknowledged her attraction to Darcy—and his to her. She would be foolish not to recognize it. But neither of them would take advantage of it until she was free. How was she ever fortunate enough to meet a man like him?

Glory was tinglingly conscious of his long, rangy body sprawled at ease next to her, of his dark, clean-cut profile and thick, crisp hair. She closed her eyes momentarily, imprinting his face on her mind's eye. Her lips tilted in a smile as she floated off to sleep, her head slowly descending to Darcy's shoulder.

He sat stiffly for a long moment before settling her more comfortably in his arms. When she snuggled closer, fitting her bright head in the curve of his neck,

Darcy drew a sharp breath. He inhaled the perfume of her hair as he stroked her back gently.

Glory frowned in her sleep, tensing at the unmistakably male touch. After a brief second she relaxed, knowing unconsciously that it wasn't Marshall. He had never touched her with tenderness. The soothing sensation wove itself into the fabric of her dreams, creating a slumberous feeling of well-being. Gradually the chemistry of her body changed, a radiant warmth and hunger spreading through it, a need emerging that had been long submerged.

With a whimper deep in her throat she cuddled closer, pressing her breasts against the hard male chest that supported her weight. When Darcy tried to put distance between them, she slid her arms around his neck, lifting her head until her lips were resting on the muscle that jerked at the point of his square jaw.

Emotion made Darcy's fingers bite more strongly into her shoulders than he intended. "Wake up, Glory," he said hoarsely.

Her eyes opened and she looked at him in confusion, noting the taut planes of his face without comprehension. Only his full, sensuous mouth filled her consciousness, those firm lips so close to her own. Without being fully aware of what she was doing, Glory urged his head down to hers, parting her lips expectantly.

Darcy's groan came from deep in his chest as his arms tightened and his mouth took full possession of hers. His tongue established a claim with a male hunger that was unmistakable, promising limitless delights that would be shared, not merely taken. He was dominant, yet giving, confident of his ability to satisfy and desirous of doing just that.

Glory felt herself melting into a fluid vessel of desire. She was filled with an excitement she had never experienced before. Her usual passive endurance disappeared, eclipsed by the blazing fire raging through her aroused body. Straining even closer, she cupped the back of Darcy's head, her fingers threading through his thick hair. Her tongue dueled with his, accepting his invitation with mindless delight.

They were lost in the wonder of each other, blind to the implications of their actions—or where they were leading. It seemed natural for Darcy's hand to curve around Glory's breast, his sensitive, stroking fingers bringing new waves of pleasure. Then he gently yet expertly unfastened the top few buttons of her shirt; his mouth slid over the exposed satin smooth skin, burning a sensuous path.

"God, you're beautiful!" he groaned, brushing his cheek slowly over the gently swelling curve of her breast.

It was as though his husky voice broke the spell she was under. Glory tensed in his arms as awareness swept over her. Darcy sensed the change immediately, attuned to her like a bow to a violin. His arms fell away and he straightened up. They looked into each other's eyes, emerald green meeting golden brown with equal consternation.

"I'm sorry," Darcy muttered. He got to his feet abruptly and went to look out the window, his back to her.

Glory fastened her buttons with shaking fingers, feeling a sense of loss even in the midst of her shame. "It was my fault as much as yours," she whispered in a barely audible voice.

Darcy didn't turn around, his rigid body showing the control he was fighting for. "I never meant this to happen, Glory."

"I know," she murmured.

"If you're ready, I'll take you home."

"Yes, I—I'll get my packages together." Her nervous fingers tucked the shirt into her jeans.

His restraint had boundaries. "Don't bother about

them now. I'll bring you back here after work tomorrow night. You can collect them then."

Glory paused in the act of smoothing her tumbled hair. "You aren't honestly still suggesting that I come to work for you?"

Darcy turned around, his face impassive. "Why not?"

"Why not?" she echoed incredulously. "After what just . . . After we . . ."

He was in control of himself now. "Listen to me, Glory. You're a very beautiful woman. I won't deny that I want you, but I promise not to mention it again until you're free. I don't consider myself excessively noble, but I do have a few scruples, and I certainly understand yours. There's no reason why we can't go on as though this never happened—unless you don't trust me."

Not trust him? After all he'd done for her? Including his restraint tonight. Darcy could have taken her easily, and it certainly wouldn't have been rape. He understood, though, and he respected her. Glory knew she would trust this man with her life. It was herself she was uncertain of.

"You know it isn't that, Darcy," she answered quietly.

A smile suddenly lightened his intense expression. "Then why are we standing around here? It's late, and I expect you at campaign headquarters at nine o'clock sharp."

He wouldn't listen to any of Glory's tentative arguments but hustled her out of the apartment and into the car with crisp efficiency. Darcy was completely relaxed once more, his easy manner relieving any tension between them. Although it wouldn't have seemed possible a short time earlier, Glory even found herself laughing with him at small jokes.

It was after she was alone in her apartment that the misgivings began to surface. A multitude of conflicting emotions swirled through her head as Glory got ready for bed. Had she allowed Darcy to persuade her so easily because she really wanted him to, wanted to go on seeing him as much as she wanted the job? And if that were the case, wasn't she being foolish? The situation between them was like a tinderbox. One spark would set it ablaze.

Except that Glory knew deep in her heart that Darcy wouldn't be the one to strike the match. Surely she could equal his restraint. If ever there was a time for self-control, this was it. For a long moment she trembled on the edge of doubt, remembering that hard, lean body, the sensual delight of his hands, the compelling passion his warm mouth evoked. Putting such forbidden pleasures firmly behind her, she settled down in the strange bed, filled with a mounting sense of anticipation. After the hideous trauma of the past months, she was finally free! A whole new life was waiting out there.

Darcy's headquarters were on Olympic Boulevard, a short bus trip away. Glory was on time to the minute, but everyone else was already there. The first person she met was Bryan Trent, Darcy's campaign manager.

Bryan was a tall, lanky young man in his early thirties. His perpetually rumpled light brown hair gave him a youthful, untried look that was deceiving. Glory was to discover that Bryan was decisive, dedicated, and intelligent. He also had a delightful sense of humor that made him great fun to be with.

His light blue eyes were admiring when Darcy introduced them. "Trust the old man to pick a coordinator who will also win him votes."

"Call me an 'old man' one more time and I'll be in the market for a new manager," Darcy warned jokingly.

"These politicians have very fragile egos," Bryan told Glory with mock solemnity.

"I'm only a candidate so far," Darcy answered dryly.

"How can you miss?" Bryan tilted his head appraisingly. "All we have to do is get out the female vote. Did you ever see such a blend of integrity and sex appeal?" he asked Glory.

Her eyes sparkled with mischief as she also surveyed Darcy. "With a little hint of unattainability mixed in. That always grabs women."

Darcy raised an eyebrow imperiously. "Did it ever occur to either of you to mention that I'm qualified for the job?"

"We'll get you elected anyway," Bryan returned, chuckling.

It was fortunate that Glory met Bryan first because her relations with the other people in the office weren't as cordial. There were two women and two men, all in their middle to late thirties. Mitchell and George greeted her with barely concealed smirks. After a comprehensive survey of Glory's physical attributes, followed by an inventory of her glowing red hair and thickly lashed green eyes, they made their conclusions —unlike Bryan, who had accepted her without question. He had been frankly admiring, but Bryan understood that her professional relationship to Darcy was just what it seemed. It would never occur to him to speculate further.

The women, Sally and Gretchen, concurred in the unvoiced opinion that Glory had gotten the job because she was Darcy's girlfriend. They were not as forbearing as the men. Added to the insult of Glory's youth was her almost flawless beauty. Although all of them were marginally polite, a troublesome situation was brewing.

Glory attempted to walk softly for the first week. She tried her best to make friends. Her efforts were met with hostility from the women and insulting behavior from the men. Since they regarded her job as merely a way for Darcy to keep his girlfriend close, they didn't consider it necessary to take her seriously.

They excluded her from logistical discussions, never telling her what they were doing or consulting her about anything. Mostly they treated her as an underling, giving her envelopes to stuff and lists of names to call.

Glory took it for just so long. At the beginning of the second week the four of them huddled in a corner, having a meeting that didn't include her. When it was concluded they grabbed their coats and headed for the door.

Glory stood up. "Hold it right there!" she ordered. "Where do you think you're going?"

The look on their faces was almost comical. "What do you mean?" George asked blankly.

Her slight figure bristled with fury. "I thought it was self-explanatory. I happen to be the coordinator here, and nobody leaves this office without telling me where they're going and when they expect to return."

"We didn't want to burden you with details," Sally said, her tone insulting.

"Burden me. It's what I'm here for," Glory answered matter-of-factly. "If any of you object to my age or my appearance, that's your problem. In spite of what you think, Darcy hired me because he thought I was competent. So far I haven't been doing my job because I've been trying to get along with all of you, but that's going to change. I'm here to see that he's elected. If the rest of you think this is just fun and games, you'll find yourselves replaced in short order. Not because I'm sleeping with the boss but because I intend to put together a professional organization. From now on you'll consult with me before you make a move; we'll discuss whether it's the right one. And at all times, I expect to know exactly what's going on." She raised her chin, looking at them disdainfully. "Is that quite clear?"

"I guess we didn't realize were were excluding you," Mitchell offered lamely.

Glory stared him down. "Well, now that you do, I

63

don't expect it to happen again." She turned to the two women. "Do you have any reservations you'd like to air? Because now's the time."

Gretchen wasn't as easily intimidated. "What's your background in politics?"

"None," Glory answered readily. "The only things I bring to this campaign are loyalty, total belief in Darcy's capabilities, and the willingness to work long hours. What is your background?"

The other woman was taken aback. "Well, I—I worked for Glen Bakstrom."

Something in her defensive attitude made Glory ask, "Were you a paid worker?"

"I don't think that makes any difference." When Glory waited pointedly, Gretchen added reluctantly, "I was a volunteer."

"Since he got elected, you must have been a good one." Glory's calm regard was neither conciliatory nor challenging. "We have a common goal. I'd like for us to work together, but it's up to you. A campaign without a coordinator is just a bunch of people spinning their wheels. I don't intend to let Darcy get sabotaged by his own organization."

The four people facing her were clearly shaken. It was as though a harmless kitten had turned into a full-grown tigress. They gazed at her silently, reluctantly reassessing her capabilities.

"Where are you all off to?" Glory demanded.

"I was going downtown to try and get an endorsement from the Commonwealth Club," Mitchell offered tentatively.

"That sounds good," Glory said crisply. "Report back here on the results. Gretchen?"

"I have a meeting with the printer about our placards and bumper stickers," she answered in a kind of daze.

Glory elicited information from the others, leaving no doubt about who was in charge. When they left the office, it was with the clear understanding that they would report back to her. Glory sank into a chair, drained from the ordeal yet knowing that what she had done was necessary.

Darcy came out of his office. His expression was amused. "Tote that barge; lift that bale."

She sprang out of her chair, ready to meet this new challenge. "If you don't approve of the way I'm handling things, I'll leave. Either I'm in charge here, or I'm not."

He ruffled her hair playfully. "I wouldn't dream of disagreeing with you. If you ever went to work for my opponent, I'd be sunk."

She looked at him doubtfully. "Do you think I came on too strong?"

He smiled beguilingly. "Do you?"

"No, I don't! Those people weren't taking me seriously. I came here to do a job, and I'm damn well going to do it if I have to get you elected single-handedly!"

"You probably could." He chuckled.

Glory's shoulders slumped suddenly. "It's no good, Darcy. This is a team effort. If they don't accept me, then I'm of no use to you." She attempted a smile to cover the hurt. "Maybe I'm not cut out for politics."

"Why don't you wait and see what happens?" Darcy suggested soothingly.

Glory braced herself for the return of the others in the afternoon. Everything depended on their reaction. They would naturally have talked things over among themselves. If they decided to present a solid hostile front, she might as well start cleaning out her desk.

Glory's calm face revealed none of her inner turmoil as Mitchell approached her late in the day.

"You wouldn't believe the reception I got at the Commonwealth Club today," he said enthusiastically. "They want Darcy to speak on the responsibility of big corporations for protecting the environment."

Glory's tension dissolved into relief and gratitude at the olive branch being extended. Mitchell was only one of four, but it was a start. She soon found the others had decided to follow suit.

The turnaround wasn't accomplished effortlessly. There was some initial embarrassment, despite good intentions on both sides. But Glory performed her part with a maturity surprising for her age, and the others both admired and appreciated it.

The first day was of course the hardest. As they trailed in, one after the other, each went to give Glory the report she had requested—demanded, actually.

"Why don't you all pull up a chair and we can begin to map our strategy," she suggested. "I'll make us some coffee."

"I'll do it," Sally offered swiftly, remembering the menial tasks they had assigned to Glory in the past.

"I don't mind." Glory smiled, moving gracefully to the coffee maker in the corner.

At no point did Darcy interfere. He merely watched from his office, his eyes resting proudly on Glory's bright head.

Getting settled in her apartment and resolving things at work had taken all of her time and energy. Even the burning question of her divorce had been put on hold, of necessity. The small breathing space turned out to be beneficial. With everything in her life on the upswing, Glory now had the confidence to face the ordeal ahead.

Breaking the news to her parents was the first hurdle.

"Where have you been, Glory? We've been out of our minds with worry ever since Marshall told us you disappeared!" her mother exclaimed.

"I'm sorry." Glory suffered real remorse. She hadn't expected Marshall to contact her parents. She honestly thought pride would keep him from revealing that she had walked out on him.

66

"How could you just up and run away from home?" her mother asked querulously.

Glory's teeth clenched in an effort at self-control. Her mother made it sound as though she were a naughty child. "That doesn't exactly describe it. I'm going to get a divorce, Mother."

"A *divorce!* You've only been married three months!"

"God knows I'm aware of that." Glory sighed, hearing for the first time the criticism that was bound to be repeated over and over.

"How can you even consider such a wicked thing? Marshall is a fine man. He loves you."

"Aren't you interested in whether I love him?" Glory asked quietly.

"Listen to me, child. Marriage isn't easy—and they do say the first year's the hardest. But you mustn't throw everything away because of a little disagreement," Mrs. Prescott advised anxiously. "I know you're not accustomed to Marshall's grand style of living. It must be a big change for you. There's no problem that can't be resolved, though, when two young people love each other."

Glory wondered what her mother would say if she told her what Marshall had tried to do to her. She was saved the impossible task when her father got on the phone.

He added his disapproval to his wife's. It was even harder parrying her dad's objections because of the underlying thread of fear in his voice. Glory knew that neither of her parents would have sacrificed her for their own welfare if they knew the truth, but that was one thing she couldn't tell them. She contented herself with reassuring her father that his job was in no way tied to her marriage. It wasn't an idle promise. Marshall would not be allowed to destroy the whole family. He wasn't above such retribution, but she would fight him on that.

* * *

After the draining conversation with her parents, the actual divorce mechanism was simple. In her meeting with the dignified lawyer Darcy recommended, Glory stated her objective simply.

"All I want from Marshall is a divorce and my maiden name back."

The older man regarded her with a carefully expressionless face. "Your husband is a very wealthy man, Mrs. Wentworth. As your attorney, I must advise you that sometimes while in an emotional state a woman decides things that she later regrets. You are entitled to sue for alimony."

"You don't understand," Glory replied impatiently. "Our marriage was a mistake from the very beginning. We were only married for three months, and I'm able-bodied. Why should Marshall pay for an error in judgment on both our parts?"

There was respect in the lawyer's eyes. "I just want to be sure you know what you're renouncing."

Glory's tense expression turned into a wide grin. "Oh, I know all right! All I want to find out is how soon I'll be free."

"We'll serve the papers immediately and file for an interlocutory decree." He smiled suddenly. "That's it."

"You mean in just a couple of days I'll be divorced?" she asked incredulously.

"Not exactly. You asked when you'd be free—from your husband, I assume. An interlocutory decree dissolves the marriage, but you can't marry anyone *else* for six months. At the end of that time, we file the final papers and you're unattached once more. In the interim, you are not Mr. Wentworth's wife unless you resume marital relations with him."

Glory was too starry-eyed at the imminent prospect of freedom to even consider the absurdity of the lawyer's last statement. A sudden thought clouded her euphoria. "Could Marshall contest the divorce?" She didn't think he'd have the gall, but there was always the chance.

Her attorney was reassuring. "In California we have something called no-fault divorce. It was initiated to speed the court calendar and do away with bitter name calling. Even when there is considerable property involved, divorces are granted without the monetary details being worked out. In your case there's no problem."

Glory floated out of his office on a cloud of happiness. All the pain and misery were coming to an end. She had made a mistake and she had paid for it. Now the future lay ahead.

Darcy was up to his eyebrows in work when she got back to the office. He was talking on two phones almost simultaneously, impatiently running his fingers through his thick hair. The top button of his shirt was undone and his sleeves were partially rolled up, revealing muscular forearms with a sprinkling of dark hair. The whole atmosphere was one of high-powered activity, with Darcy in complete command.

Glory watched him through the glass partition, a multitude of emotions racing through her. He was the most compelling man she had ever met—and soon he wouldn't be off limits.

Darcy glanced up absently. Something about her attitude registered, and he got rid of his callers swiftly. Coming out of the office, he approached Glory, putting his hands on her shoulders while he looked at her with a slight frown.

"Is anything wrong, Glory?"

The smile she gave him quieted all his fears. "Not a thing in this world. How would you like to come to dinner at my place a week from tonight?" she asked with a lilt in her voice.

CHAPTER FOUR

Glory's visit to the attorney put a smile on her face that lasted all day. It was still there when she got home that night. From this moment on, Marshall was a part of the past. She was rid of him at last and was ready to start a new life.

As she walked to her apartment from the bus stop Ellen Dressler was just pulling up to the house. They had met occasionally when Darcy was helping Glory get settled, but each time the other woman had merely nodded coldly and gone on by. It would have been nice to be friends, but Glory accepted the fact the Ellen had taken a dislike to her for some reason. Ordinarily she would have settled for a restrained hello when they met going up the walk. That day, however, Glory was bubbling over with goodwill toward the world.

She smiled radiantly. "Wasn't it a glorious day?"

Her gaiety was infectious. Ellen smiled back. "It certainly must have been for you."

The pleasant expression made her look like an entirely different person. Glory noticed for the first time that Ellen was really quite attractive. Her mouth was wide and generous when it wasn't tightly compressed, and there was a sparkle in her velvety brown eyes.

"This was probably the best day of my whole life," Glory agreed.

"Did you come into a fortune or something?"

"No, I got rid of one."

"That sounds definitely provocative," Ellen said with

a tentative laugh. "You aren't going to leave me hanging, are you? How would you like to come in for some iced tea? Unless you're in a hurry to get ready for a date." A hint of her former austere manner returned.

"No, I'm free as a bird," Glory said. "I'd love some iced tea."

Ellen's apartment was very similar to Glory's. Both had the same air of faded elegance that was part of the charm. As Glory followed her neighbor into the kitchen she said, "I'm not keeping *you* from anything, am I?"

"I have a choice between washing my hair or cleaning closets tonight," Ellen answered dryly. "That ought to tell you what a fascinating life I lead."

"Have you lived in Los Angeles long?" Glory asked. A woman as attractive as Ellen should have a lot of dates. Perhaps she hadn't met anyone yet because she was a newcomer.

"Too long," Ellen answered curtly, disproving that theory. "I sometimes wonder why I stay. My job, I guess. I hate to give up all I've worked for—along with everything else," she added, contributing to the mystery.

"Where are you from?" That seemed a safe enough question.

"A little town in Michigan. That's where all my family and friends are."

"Did you go to college here? Is that how you happened to relocate?" Glory didn't mean to pry, but there was something very puzzling about Ellen.

"No." Her curt answer didn't invite further questions.

There was a brief silence while Ellen got out ice cubes and spooned instant tea into tall glasses. As Glory was wondering if it had been a mistake to accept the invitation, Ellen began to show signs of regretting her coolness.

Her face cleared as she set a glass in front of Glory

and sat down at the table opposite her. "So . . . tell me about that fortune you gave away. I wish I'd been there."

It was Glory's turn to be reticent. She had no desire to air her dirty linen, but it would probably come out anyway. It was very possible that the newspapers would have a field day with the whole sorry mess if they got wind of the divorce. Ellen was bound to find out sooner or later.

"I started divorce proceedings today," Glory said quietly.

Whatever Ellen had expected, that wasn't it. "From the man who helped you move in?" she asked with evident surprise.

"No, Darcy is . . . He's just a friend."

"That's a laugh! Men want a lot of things from women, but friendship isn't even on the shopping list. Is he the next matrimonial candidate?" Ellen's mouth twisted sardonically.

"Of course not!" It was important that Glory correct her misconception. "Darcy is exactly what I said—a very good friend. He helped me through the worst period of my life."

Ellen shrugged. "If you say so."

"I just did!" Glory looked at the other woman in frustration. "Why do you find that so hard to believe?"

"Because I know men," Ellen answered bluntly. "If he did something for you, it was for reasons of his own." She gazed cynically at Glory's vibrant hair and exquisite features. "Do you think he'd have done the same thing if you were fat and fifty?"

"*Yes!* You don't know anything about Darcy Lord."

"I knew a man very much like him. He was handsome and macho, too—a real hunk. Women couldn't stay away from him, and vice versa. Oh, he had a real knack, just like your Darcy." Ellen's hand clenched around her glass. "When you were with him he swore

72

that you were the only woman he had ever loved. And we all believed him." Her smile was bitter.

Glory was startled by the intensity of Ellen's feeling. She had evidently been hurt badly. "I guess we all meet losers like that at sometime in our lives," she said lamely.

"But I married him."

"Oh—I—I'm sorry." Glory didn't know what else to say.

"Think how *I* feel." Ellen's smile had a hint of its old gaiety.

"Would you like to talk about it?"

"Why not? If we're going to be friends, we might as well clear the air," Ellen said matter-of-factly. "I fell in love with Jordan on our first date. We met at a party, and I couldn't believe my luck when he asked me out. Maybe somebody told him I had a good job," she added derisively. "He wasn't working, but he took me to all the best places. Jordan was the last of the big time spenders, and why not? It wasn't his money. I found out later that he owed everyone in town."

"Didn't he ever work?"

"When it didn't interfere with his social life. He was a used car salesman, and he could always get a job if it came to that. The funny thing is that he could have made big money if he'd put even half his energy into it. But that would have meant curtailing his matinees with married ladies while *their* husbands were working."

"How long did you go together before you were married?"

"Just a few weeks. Not long enough to find out anything about him. I was so dazzled that I probably wouldn't have believed the truth anyway. As I said, he was quite a charmer."

Glory hesitated. "Why did . . . I mean, he doesn't sound like the marrying kind."

"Why did he marry *me* is what you meant."

73

"No! I—"

"It's all right. Everyone else wondered the same thing. After all, I'm not exactly a raving beauty." Ellen's voice was filled with self-mockery.

"You mustn't put yourself down like that," Glory scolded. "I just wondered why he'd want a wife. It must have meant making a lot of excuses."

"Jordan could have written a book on excuses," Ellen said tersely. "He married me because his creditors were starting to close in and he had to lie low for a while. I was a combined meal ticket and bed partner, although God knows he had enough of those. His girlfriends got perfume and black lace nightgowns; I got the bills. It was a shock to discover that I was still liable for his debts after I divorced him."

Glory was appalled. "That's outrageous!"

"It was worth it to get rid of him. But now maybe you'll understand why your Darcy Lord leaves me cold."

"That's not fair," Glory protested. "You had a ghastly experience, but it doesn't mean that all men are rotten."

"How about *your* husband? I don't imagine you're divorcing him because he didn't fold his napkin properly."

Glory's eyes fell. "Marshall wasn't any prize either."

"What did I tell you!"

"Listen to me, Ellen," Glory said earnestly. "In my own way, I had an experience every bit as bad as yours. But I'm not willing to condemn half the human race because of two rotten apples."

"You'd rather wait until you get food poisoning? Wise up, Glory!" Ellen went on impatiently. "Men are all alike. You can trust them about as far as you can see on a foggy night."

"I realize I'm not going to convince you, but some-

74

day you'll meet a man who will. A kind, decent man like Darcy."

"Sure, and the tooth fairy puts money under your pillow when you lose a baby molar. Well, fortunately my wisdom teeth finally came in. I no longer believe in fairy tales. If you're smart you'll put them under file and forget, too."

By tacit consent they changed the subject after that. On other matters they found themselves in frequent agreement. A budding friendship was formed by the time Glory went back to her own apartment. Ellen's attitude toward Darcy troubled her, but she hoped her neighbor would come around when she got to know him. Just thinking about Darcy brought a smile back to Glory's face.

The next week was hectic but rewarding. All the awkwardness between Glory and her coworkers gradually disappeared. They were functioning like a well-oiled machine as the campaign shifted into high gear. Darcy was in such demand that they could have used a dozen more workers, but no one minded doing double duty. Glory was especially busy because her duties were so varied.

Darcy came out of his office one day as she was sorting precinct lists into different piles. It was one of the rare occasions when everyone else was out of the office. Glory had the phone cradled on her shoulder, taking a call without pausing in her other work.

When she hung up, Darcy said, "Slow down, little one. No one expects you to work yourself to a frazzle."

She gave him a brilliant smile. "This isn't work. I had no idea that electing a state senator would be so much fun."

"Hasn't anyone ever told you not to count your chickens?"

"It's on the barbecue, ready to be served up to an appreciative public," she replied, grinning.

"The barbecue is the only part I agree with." His firm mouth turned down at the corners. "I get grilled every day from one segment of the population or the other. It's amazing how many special interest groups there are."

"But you won't give in to them," Glory stated. "That's why everyone is going to vote for you—because they know you're the best man for the job."

Darcy frowned slightly as he looked down at her animated face. "It's nice to be optimistic, honey, but you mustn't bank on this thing. It's almost three months until the election. A lot could happen before then."

"I trust you not to walk in front of a bus or fall off your penthouse terrace. That's the only way you could lose the election."

Darcy sighed. "I hope for your sake you're not disappointed."

"I'm not the one who's running!" Glory's smooth brow wrinkled. "Wouldn't it bother you to lose?"

"Of course it would. I'm used to fighting every inch of the way. I want very much to be state senator, but it wouldn't destroy me if the decision goes the other way. Especially if I lost because I refused to compromise my principles or give up my private life."

"I don't think politicians have much privacy."

"They sure don't during the campaign!" A different kind of intensity lighted Darcy's eyes. His voice dropped to a husky pitch. "I never get to see you anymore."

Glory felt a glow start deep in her midsection. "You see me every day," she murmured.

He smoothed the shining hair off her forehead in a tantalizing caress. "That wasn't what I had in mind. Didn't you say something about dinner?"

"Funny you should mention it." She laughed breathlessly. "I was going to ask you if you'd like to come over tomorrow night." When he hesitated for just a moment, she said hurriedly, "We can make it another time if you're busy."

"No, tomorrow night is fine. Important things deserve top priority." Darcy's slow smile made her heart beat erratically. "Bryan will just have to rearrange my schedule."

Glory left work early the next day in order to do her marketing. She was grateful for all the convenience foods available—she didn't have time to do everything from scratch. The steaks could be done at the last minute, but the potatoes would have to go in the oven earlier, along with the frozen spinach soufflé.

Glory checked her basket one last time. There were sour cream and chives for the baked potatoes, ice cream, and a jar of dark sweet cherries for the cherries jubilee that she would flame at the table. That should do it.

After she put her groceries away Glory set the table. She had remembered to buy candles but not flowers. The table needed a centerpiece, which was no problem; there were beautiful roses in the garden outside. Glory felt sure that Mrs. Belmont wouldn't mind if she cut some, but she didn't want to do it without asking. It meant a trip upstairs to see her sometimes long-winded landlady, and Glory really couldn't spare the time. After dinner was started she had to shower and change clothes. It seemed worth it, though, to have everything just right.

"Of course, take as many as you like," Mrs. Belmont said. "I'll lend you my silver epergne to put them in. Oh, and my coffee service, too."

"Thanks, but that isn't necessary," Glory protested.

"Nonsense, child. There's nothing so gracious as coffee in the living room after dinner. I'll never forget a dinner party I gave when I was your age. Someone brought this absolutely fascinating man—he even had a title. Isn't that delicious?"

Glory tactfully tried to cut the story short, but she was running late by the time she went downstairs to her apartment. Discovering that she'd forgotten to buy butter didn't help. She cast a despairing eye at the clock and went across the hall to knock on Ellen's door.

After she explained, Ellen said, "Sure, come in the kitchen." She grinned at Glory over her shoulder. "If you promise not to eat any, I'll lace it with a little arsenic."

"I wouldn't advise it," Glory warned. "With your kind of luck you'd get an all-male jury."

"Isn't that the truth?" Ellen replied sadly.

Glory rushed through her shower, but she took time over her makeup. She usually wore very little, but this was a special occasion. It was actually her first real date with Darcy. Her eyes were very bright as she sat at the flounced dressing table in just a pair of bikini panties and high-heeled sandals. The blue silk caftan she would wear was thrown across the bed.

Glory's hand shook slightly as she applied iridescent blue eyeshadow that matched the filmy caftan. Tonight's dinner could be very significant. She knew that Darcy was interested in her, but was it just a sexual attraction? He had been unbelievably kind when she was in trouble, never trying to take advantage of her. But now that she was free of Marshall it was a different story. Darcy was a man, after all, and a very virile one. He would be a wonderful lover, she knew instinctively, but was that what she really wanted?

Glory's reflection stared back from the mirror. Her green eyes in their frame of long thick lashes looked troubled. What *was* she looking for? Certainly not another husband. Yet definitely not a casual affair either. She slowly outlined her full mouth with a lip brush,

78

trying to sort out her feelings. Darcy affected her like no other man she had ever met. But was it just a physical attraction for her, too?

That wasn't enough, she decided as she gathered her long bright hair in both hands and pinned it to her crown. It cascaded down in a shining mass of waves and ringlets, with little curls escaping at the nape of her neck. Perhaps some women could sleep with a man for mere physical release, but she wasn't one of them. Glory didn't want any man to use *her* that way either. Marshall had only wanted to possess her body. That should be enough of an object lesson, although to compare the two men was laughable.

The doorbell rang, putting an end to her soul searching. Glory grabbed her caftan and stepped into it. In her haste she caught the back zipper in the waistband of her bikini panties. While she struggled to free it, the bell rang again. With a despairing groan she held the two edges together in the back and ran for the door.

"You're early," she said breathlessly.

"No, I'm exactly on time." He smiled, holding out a bottle of wine. When she kept her arms in back of her without reaching for the bottle, Darcy asked, "Is anything wrong?"

She gritted her teeth. "I can't get my zipper unstuck."

"Let me try."

As he turned her around Glory pulled the two sides of the caftan together, very conscious of the fact that she was bare all the way down to her hips.

"Let's get a little light on the subject." Darcy led her over to a chair by a lamp. He sat down and pulled her gently between his legs. "You really did a job on this."

"I was trying to hurry," she muttered.

"I would have waited." His knuckles slid up and down along her lower spine.

Glory didn't know if it was accidental or not. She

79

only knew that his intimate touch on her bare skin was making her legs tremble. "Maybe I'd better change into something else," she said faintly.

Darcy's arm circled her waist and pulled her back as she started to move away. "Don't be so impatient. That's how you got into this fix in the first place."

She was forced to stand there, feeling his warm breath on her back. By the time the zipper slid freely and he turned her to face him, Glory's whole body seemed on fire.

Darcy was wearing a broad grin. "I told you I was a handy man to have around. Is there anything else I can do for you?"

"I can't think of anything." She tried to match his light tone, but it was an effort. Glory was very conscious of being pinned between his muscular thighs. When she put her hands on his shoulders to steady herself, their solid masculine bulk made her even more vulnerable.

Darcy felt the tremor that went through her. "Are you sure, Glory?"

His hands slid from her waist up her rib cage, tantalizingly close to her swelling breasts. With a slight pressure he guided her down to his lap. One arm circled her shoulders, while the other went around her waist. Their faces were so close that she felt scorched by the flames in his golden brown eyes. As Darcy's head bent to hers, Glory's lips parted instinctively.

A loud noise suddenly shattered the quivering silence. It rasped on endlessly, like someone leaning on a buzzer, demanding attention. Glory stared at Darcy in a daze for a moment, unable to return to reality.

Finally she murmured, "It's the oven timer."

"Let it ring," he growled.

But it wasn't possible. The mood was destroyed. She got to her feet and hurried into the kitchen. Glory's emotions were in such a turmoil that she couldn't decide whether she was glad for the interruption or provoked by it. She turned off the stove with a shaking hand.

When Darcy followed her she couldn't look at him. "Fix yourself a drink while I get everything organized," she said over her shoulder.

He moved very close. "Is that what you really want, Glory?"

How could she tell him when she didn't know the answer herself? Her body clamored for one thing, whereas her clearing mind urged caution. There were so many reasons to wait—to be sure that she wasn't just a passing fancy to Darcy.

He certainly wasn't the Don Juan type who had to bed every woman as a matter of principle, yet his intentions at that moment were quite clear. Ellen's warning echoed in Glory's ears in spite of her conviction that Darcy was different from other men.

He watched the troubled thoughts coursing across her expressive face. Darcy's smile was rueful. "Some men are saved by the bell; I was knocked out by it. Okay, honey, I'll fix drinks."

Glory finally managed to relax over dinner. That, at least, had turned out perfectly. The table looked lovely with its centerpiece of pink and white roses and tall candles. The steak was done to perfection, and the cherries jubilee flamed glamorously.

Darcy contributed to the success of the meal by exerting his considerable charm in a nonthreatening way. It was as if the brief, emotion-charged episode between them had never occurred. After dinner they took their coffee into the living room and sat on the couch together.

"You have to expect silly questions when you speak in front of large groups," Glory said, continuing their conversation on the annoying things people ask.

81

He raised a peaked eyebrow. "Like have I ever been married . . . What's that got to do with anything?"

Glory laughed. "The woman who asked that probably wanted to know if you were: A, presently married; B, paying alimony. It makes a difference in a man's eligibility."

"How do you know it was a woman who asked?"

"A man would be more interested in what kind of car you drive."

"I hope you realize that those are both sexual stereotypes," Darcy said with mock severity.

"Not at all. You must admit that women look at a handsome man differently than another man would."

"I'm flattered by the compliment."

"Let's have no false modesty. Bryan and I keep telling you the women's vote is going to put you over the top," she teased.

"I haven't demonstrated such great irresistibility where you're concerned," Darcy commented dryly.

Glory perceived that they were heading for dangerous ground. She tried to change direction. "Sure you have," she replied lightly. "Haven't I told you that I don't know what I would have done without you?"

"I'm not talking about gratitude," he said quietly. "If there was ever any debt, you've more than repaid it. Why are you so wary of me, Glory? Is it because of that rotten little slug you were married to? Has he made you afraid of all men?" Darcy's strong jaw set grimly.

"No, it isn't that," Glory replied hastily. It was lucky that Darcy didn't know just *how* irresistible he was! "I realize that Marshall isn't representative of the whole male sex, thank the Lord!"

"Then it must be something about me. Whenever the laughter stops, you get nervous." He stared at her somberly. "You don't honestly think I'd force myself on you?"

"Oh, Darcy, no! It isn't that at all! This is just so new

to me." She gave him a lopsided smile. "It's been a long time since I've had a date."

His stern expression lightened. "They haven't changed that much. Men and women still enjoy each other's company."

Glory examined her nails with great care. "There's a little more to it than that."

He took both of her hands in his large, capable ones. "Why does it bother you so that we're attracted to each other? It's been obvious from the moment we met."

"But I was married then," she muttered.

"And now you think I consider you fair game because you're divorced?"

"No! It—it does make a difference, though."

Darcy's hands tightened as she started to pull hers away. "Listen to me, honey. I'd be lying if I said I didn't want to make love to you. You're a very beautiful, desirable woman. I'd like to show you the way it can be between a man and a woman—the way it *should* be. Your pleasure is as important to me as my own. Maybe it's too soon for you to believe that, considering the bad experience you've had. But someday you're going to trust me, and it's going to be so good between us."

His low voice seemed to vibrate deep inside her, sending tiny embers racing through her bloodstream. She could imagine how it would be. Darcy would make love to her with passion and tenderness, carrying her to heights she'd never climbed before. Glory's breathing was ragged as she stared into his eyes.

"Someday, sweetheart," he repeated, bending his head to kiss her gently on the lips.

It was the utter sweetness of his gesture that crept under her defenses. If he had been openly seductive, she would have resisted automatically, but Darcy's restraint touched her. As he started to draw back, Glory's arms circled his neck. Her fingers smoothed his thick dark hair, pulling his head down again.

Darcy's arms tightened around her. "My sweet little darling," he murmured before his mouth closed over hers.

He parted her lips for a male exploration that left Glory clinging to him. It was a sensuous possession, promising even greater delights. She pressed against him, restlessly kneading the width of his shoulders, the bunched muscles of his back.

"You're so lovely," he whispered, groaning.

His hands explored her body as she was exploring his. But after he traced the line of tiny bones down to her waist, his hand moved up her side to curl around her breast. Glory drew a sharp breath as his thumb circled her sensitive nipple. It hardened under his slow, devastating caress, sending an urgent signal through her entire body. She arched against his hand and dug her nails into his back.

"Darcy," she breathed.

"I know, my darling," he answered softly.

Glory felt as though she would burst into flames as he unfastened the zipper at the back of her caftan. His fingers seemed to scorch a path of fire on her already heated skin. She trembled in his arms, reaching for the rapture she knew he was about to give her.

The doorbell was a rude intrusion in their private Eden. They stared at each other in shock.

"Were you expecting someone?" Darcy asked in a low voice.

"No, I can't imagine . . ." Glory moved out of his arms self-consciously.

"I suppose you have to answer it." He sighed as the bell rang again. "Whoever it is can see the lights."

"Yes." She fastened her zipper and smoothed her hair nervously on the way to the door.

Mrs. Belmont stood in the hallway holding a plate of

strawberry tarts. She wore a long printed chiffon gown suitable for an old-fashioned garden party, and her hair was caught back with a diamond comb. "I do hope you haven't had dessert yet." She held the plate out to Glory. "I made these especially for your dinner party."

"Well, we've already—" Glory stopped herself. "How very kind of you."

"Not at all, my dear. I didn't have anything else to do," the older woman said with a faint sigh.

It was obvious that Mrs. Belmont hoped to be invited in. That was the reason for the dressy gown. Glory didn't have the heart to disappoint her after all the trouble she had gone to. "Won't you come in for coffee?" she asked, trying to sound as though she meant it.

"That would be perfectly delightful if you're sure I'm not intruding."

Darcy glanced mischievously at Glory as he rose to greet the old lady. "Wherever would you get an idea like that? We had just about run out of conversation."

Glory didn't share his amusement. How could he turn off his emotions that easily when she was still as tightly coiled as a spool of thread? With a murmured excuse she went into the kitchen for another cup and saucer. It gave her a chance to pull herself together and sort out her feelings.

If there hadn't been an interruption, she would be lying in Darcy's arms right now. Was someone up there trying to save her from making a big mistake? Glory remembered her earlier doubts. And then she remembered Darcy's gentleness, the way he hadn't pressured her. She had been the one who initiated their lovemaking; he had been willing to wait. That said a lot about his character.

Suddenly all of her uncertainty was resolved. Darcy was a rare kind of man. He would never hurt her intentionally. Maybe she felt more strongly about him than he did about her, but that was just a chance she'd have to take. Standing on the sidelines of life wasn't really living.

When she returned to the front room, her guests were deep in conversation—or rather, Mrs. Belmont was talking and Darcy was listening. He looked up with a special smile for Glory. When she returned it in kind, something electric leapt between them.

"I was telling Darcy where I got the tart recipe." Mrs. Belmont paused in her story to bring Glory up-to-date. "There was this wonderful chef at a simply marvelous restaurant. He was a true artist but *so* temperamental! Well, anyway . . ."

Glory curled up in a big chair across from the two on the couch, not really listening. Mrs. Belmont's stories didn't require comments, so she was free to gaze at Darcy to her heart's content. He looked relaxed and he appeared to be giving the older woman his full attention, but every now and then, he exchanged a glance full of promise with Glory.

It was good of him not to show his impatience, she reflected. The old lady really was lonely. Mrs. Belmont lived only vicariously now. Glory tried to match Darcy's patience. She looked at his lithe body, remembering the throbbing feeling of being molded along its hard length. Glory closed her eyes for a moment to relive the experience as her landlady's voice droned on.

The next thing she knew was a light tap on the shoulder and Mrs. Belmont's voice saying, "You'd better get to bed, young lady. You must be exhausted to fall asleep in a chair like that. Come along, Darcy. This child needs her rest. I'll lock the front door behind you."

"Oh, no!" Glory sprang to her feet. "I'm not a bit tired! You don't have to go." Her dismayed eyes met Darcy's rueful ones.

"How do you expect to get up for work tomorrow?" the old lady scolded, beckoning firmly to Darcy. She paused at the door with a twinkle in her eyes. "You can kiss each other good night. I won't look."

Darcy put his hands on Glory's shoulders and gazed down at her with a tender smile. "I guess it just wasn't our night," he murmured in her ear before kissing her gently on the lips. It was a kiss full of longing, almost unbearably sweet.

When he lifted his head she whispered, "I'm sorry."

"You're worth waiting for," he answered softly.

As she carried the coffee cups into the kitchen Glory tried to tell herself that at least they'd made an old lady happy that night. The thought wasn't as uplifting as it should have been.

CHAPTER FIVE

Glory felt shy with Darcy in the office the next day. It was difficult to look at him without recalling her passionate response the night before. The recollection was in his eyes, too, although it didn't show in his manner. Fortunately the usual bedlam reigned, and they were soon too busy for personal matters.

It was a normal day, with constantly ringing phones and crises that arose and were resolved. Glory dealt with everything calmly and efficiently. She really enjoyed the boiler room atmosphere.

It was late in the day when Bryan came to her with a worried frown on his pleasant face. "I have a big favor to ask, Glory. I know it's last minute, but could you possibly take my place at that fund-raiser tonight? Someone has to run interference for Darcy. People always want to monopolize the candidate, and he's so polite that he doesn't know how to cut anyone short. It isn't good politics anyway. Somebody else has to do it for him. Do you think you could manage?"

"Sure, I'd be glad to." Glory tried to keep the eagerness out of her voice.

"You have to be firm," Bryan warned. "It won't win you any brownie points, but it's important to keep him circulating." He looked worried. "I hate to skip out, but my housekeeper got sick. I have to pick up Steffie at nursery school and make dinner for her."

Glory knew that Bryan was raising a four-year-old

daughter by himself. "Don't worry about a thing. I'll be glad to take over."

Everything conspired to keep her late at the office that day, so Glory set a record for getting ready. It didn't show, however. By the time Darcy rang the bell, she had showered and changed into a white silk gown that clung to her curved body in all the right places. A necklace of carved green beads matched the sparkle in her emerald eyes. Because of the shortage of time, she had simply brushed her red hair until it shone and left it to curl around her creamy shoulders.

Darcy's eyes flamed at the sight of her. "Did you have to look so beautiful?" His hand smoothed the silky length of her hair. "I wonder what would happen if we showed up an hour late?"

Glory forced down her own rising desire. "Bryan would certainly have a heart attack. Do you want that on your conscience?"

"I suppose not. But does it strike you that we're always making someone else happy at the expense of our own satisfaction?" he asked plaintively.

"They say virtue is its own reward." Even as Glory took refuge in joking, she remembered saying that to Darcy once before when they were in a similarly intimate situation.

"Don't you believe it! Virtue isn't even in the running with the kind of satisfaction I have in mind." His husky voice curled around her like a caress.

"We'd better go," she said hastily. "Bryan will have my scalp if I don't get you there on time."

Darcy gathered her long hair in one hand, gently tugging her head back so he could smile down at her. "You win. It's much too pretty a head to lose."

The grand ballroom of the Century Plaza Hotel was packed, which was very satisfying. This was a major fund-raiser. Darcy was surrounded as soon as they entered the big room, and Glory began to see why he needed an aide. Everyone vied for his attention. Some asked assurance that he was on their side of an issue, others wanted favors, and many just hoped celebrity would rub off on them.

Glory tried to keep him moving through the crowd so everyone got a few minutes of his time. She was hampered by not knowing exactly who the big wheels were, but she could see that most of the women who tried to monopolize Darcy were clearly interested in something other than politics.

Glory's soft mouth set grimly as she was forced to watch the number of beautiful women who tried to get him alone. It would have been different if Darcy had been merely polite, but he wasn't. It seemed to Glory that he responded above and beyond the call of duty to those silly females.

"You'll have to excuse us," she said briskly to a gorgeous blond who was hanging on Darcy's arm. Her beaded gown would have paid the rent on their campaign headquarters for two months. "Mr. Lord has to get to the head table."

He smiled down at Glory's grim face as she led him away. "You look as though you just bit into a persimmon. Didn't you like Mrs. Courtland?"

"Not as much as you did," she answered curtly. "Besides, Bryan told me not to let anyone corner you."

"You're both determined to see that I don't have any fun, aren't you?" he teased.

"You're not here to have fun," she replied primly. "You're running for election."

"If I thought the two were mutually incompatible, I'd pull out of the race."

Before Glory could answer, another stunning woman blocked their path. "I want you to know you have the support of our whole country club, Mr. Lord." Her sexy voice was a breathless imitation of Marilyn

Monroe's. "Would you come to one of our dinner dances? We have them every Saturday night."

He took the hand she offered in both of his. "I'd consider it an honor." Darcy's voice would have melted steel.

"When?" she asked urgently.

"Why don't you phone headquarters for a time?" Glory cut in smoothly. "Bryan Trent takes care of Mr. Lord's appearances." She steered him away deftly, trying to contain her anger.

"Very well done," he whispered in her ear. "You're even better at this than Bryan."

"Didn't you want to go?" She frowned at him. "You certainly gave that impression."

"I'm learning." His smile was slightly smug.

Glory did her job mechanically for the rest of the cocktail hour. If Darcy could put on that good an act, how could anyone tell when he was really sincere? It was a sobering thought.

When dinner was over, Darcy made a rousing speech. There was no doubt about where he stood on the issues anyway. By the time he finished talking Glory was bursting with pride. She stood on the sidelines as people came up to pump his hand and pledge their support.

When the music started, Darcy led her onto the floor. "Did it go all right?" he asked.

"You were brilliant," she answered simply. "There wasn't a whisper while you were speaking."

"In spite of the fact that I didn't mince any words?"

"Because of it," she assured him. "People might not agree with everything you say, but they respect a man who stands up for what he believes in."

"That's the only way I want to be elected." His handsome face was completely serious. "I want this job, Glory, but I don't need it. I won't compromise one inch to get it."

"You don't have to, Mr. Senator." Her smile was enchanting. "Even the men are going to vote for you."

"You little devil! How can I convince you that sex appeal isn't on the ballot?"

As she gazed up into his smiling face, Glory knew that Darcy could convince her of anything. Was she just as foolish as all those other women who chased after him and heard only what they wanted to hear? Glory knew in her heart that she was building paper dragons again. But the competition *was* formidable. How long could one woman hope to hold his interest when there were so many waiting in the wings?

Darcy gazed down at her suddenly troubled expression. "Hey, what did I say wrong? Did you suddenly realize that my opponents might be considered sexier?"

"Nobody can compare with you," she said simply, dropping all pretense for a moment.

His arms tightened, folding her so closely that she could feel his heartbeat. "That means more to me than all the empty compliments I've received tonight. You're very special to me, Glory. You know that, don't you?"

"I hope so," she whispered.

His lips brushed against her temple. "Let's get out of this place so I can show you."

Darcy led her off the dance floor. As they threaded their way to the exit, he was stopped constantly. Everyone wanted to congratulate him on his speech and talk about the issues. Glory resigned herself to the fact that it was going to take a long time to get out of there. She didn't know just *how* long. As they inched toward freedom Bryan suddenly appeared.

"What are you doing here!" Glory exclaimed.

"I finally managed to locate a sitter. How's it going?"

"You didn't have to do that, Bryan. Everything's fine."

"I was sure it would be. Darcy's a pro—even without experience," he said admiringly. "And I knew you

92

could handle things," Bryan added hastily. "I just thought I'd drop by to lend a hand."

"It was really a waste of time," Glory told him. "We were just leaving."

"Leaving?" Bryan looked at his watch. "Darcy can't cut out now! There's a whole hour of dancing ahead. He has to waltz some of the V.I.P. wives around. Has he danced with Mrs. Courtland yet, or J. J. Harrison's wife?"

"Well, I . . . No, I don't believe so."

Bryan clucked his tongue disapprovingly. "He'd better get on the ball."

When Darcy finally disentangled himself from the group surrounding him, he greeted Bryan with surprise. "I thought you were tied up tonight. Who's taking care of Steffie?"

"I got a sitter—it's a good thing, too. Glory tells me you were leaving."

"Well, uh—there didn't seem to be any reason to stick around any longer."

Bryan looked briefly at the ceiling. "How about dancing with the wives of your most important backers?"

Darcy's jaw set stubbornly. "There seems to be a bit of confusion here as to just what kind of job I'm running for. I don't aspire to be male centerfold of the month."

"Be reasonable," Bryan pleaded. "If you were married, it would be different. But since you're not, the ladies expect a little harmless attention—especially when their husbands have contributed thousands of dollars to your campaign."

"That's not the way I intend to do the job if I'm elected, so why should I run my campaign that way?" Darcy asked austerely.

"I'm not asking you to take them up on anything. Heaven forbid! All we need is a breath of scandal."

Bryan shook his head. "It would sink us faster than the iceberg that clobbered the Titanic!"

"Then you won't have any objections if Glory and I leave now," Darcy observed dryly.

"You can't," Bryan insisted. "Look, Darcy, I know how you feel and I agree with you. It would be nice if we didn't have to go through all the glad-handing and the meaningless get-togethers if the best man won solely on merit. But we both know that isn't how it's done. If you really want to get elected so you can accomplish some reforms, you'll follow the rules, no matter how stupid they are."

Darcy looked undecided. "I told Glory we were leaving."

She was touched by his indecision, but she couldn't let him antagonize his backers for her. "Bryan's right," she said hastily. "I should have realized it myself. It's a good thing he got here in time."

"Yes, aren't we lucky?" Darcy answered sardonically. His eyes sought hers in apology.

She tried to convey the message that none was needed, but they both felt a sense of frustration.

Bryan took over, demonstrating to Glory how much she had to learn. He guided Darcy to the most important groups and steered Glory toward the lesser ones. When he introduced them, he skillfully included background information on their interests so she had something to work with.

Glory displayed a hidden aptitude for the job. She found ways to be flattering without being insincere, which made her efforts more effective. It got to be quite enjoyable.

Glory was less happy when she glimpsed Darcy's dark head poised over one lovely partner after another. Was he being sincere, too? Did their blond or dark beauty really appeal to him? The interest on his handsome face seemed genuine. Could he be that captivated if his true feelings were for someone else? Glory's pleasure in the evening suddenly diminished.

It was late when Bryan decided they had finally fulfilled their obligations. Glory's high-heeled sandals were biting into her instep, and her smile seemed permanently fixed.

"Don't tell me we can go home now?" she asked Bryan mockingly. "I thought we were spending the weekend here."

"It felt like it," Darcy agreed, sighing. "I must have steered three dozen matrons around the dance floor."

"I didn't notice you dancing with anyone exactly doddering," Glory said caustically.

"The young ones are the most aggressive," he complained. "It makes you wonder what's wrong with their husbands."

"It's not your problem," Bryan warned.

"That's true. I have problems of my own." Darcy's golden brown eyes held Glory's. "Very frustrating ones."

"No, you don't," Bryan assured him. "I've been circulating tonight and the response has been absolutely fantastic. Everyone says the election is in the bag."

"To paraphrase Mark Twain, the reports of my election are greatly exaggerated," Darcy remarked dryly.

"Well, sure, something unforeseen could happen," Bryan admitted, "but it would have to be strictly out of left field."

"Would you mind saving your predictions for the strategy meeting tomorrow?" Darcy asked. "Glory's tired and I want to get her home before she falls asleep." He gave her a melting smile. "She's been known to do that at the most inconvenient times."

The corners of her lips twitched. It was funny in retrospect, although it hadn't been at the time. "At least you got a good night's sleep, too."

Darcy raised one eyebrow. "Is that what you really think?"

The significance behind their banter went over Bryan's head, since they always joked around together in the office. That's what Glory counted on.

"I think we could all use a few hours of shut-eye," Bryan said. "It's been a long day."

"Right." Darcy took Glory's arm and led her toward the door for the second time that evening.

When they reached the motor entrance, Bryan held out his hand. "Give me your claim checks, and I'll give them to the parking attendant."

Darcy held out one ticket. "Glory is with me."

Bryan looked surprised. "You came all the way across town to pick her up?"

"I don't have a car," she explained.

"That's really rough in this town," Bryan said. "You ought to give some thought to getting one."

"It takes more than thought." She smiled impishly. "Since it was your idea, how about arranging a raise for a very deserving coworker?"

He grinned back at her. "On second thought, a car can be a royal pain. Fighting all that traffic instead of sitting comfortably on a bus."

Glory laughed. "I never knew you were so thoughtful."

"When it comes to doling out the boss's money, I'm thinking every minute."

Darcy hadn't taken any part in the conversation. He stood there jingling some coins in his pocket while he scanned the driveway impatiently. Suddenly his face cleared. "Here's your car."

"And there's yours," Bryan said as Darcy's silver Mercedes convertible was driven up in back of his more modest Toyota. "We'll see you tomorrow." He took Glory's arm.

"I'll take Glory home!" Darcy said sharply.

"No problem—I go right by her house," Bryan answered.

Darcy had trouble controlling his annoyance. "She doesn't live in outer Mongolia. It isn't that much out of my way."

"What's the point, though? As long as she has a ride home." Bryan's face suddenly clouded. "Unless you don't trust me to get her there safely."

"Of course he does!" Glory broke in hastily. "Darcy is just being a gentleman. He thinks he has an obligation to take me home since he picked me up."

"Listen, Sir Galahad, you just put in a fifteen-hour day. Glory doesn't expect company manners. Did you finish that speech for the League of Women Voters?" Bryan asked suddenly.

Darcy's irritation threatened to get out of hand. "What are you, my conscience?"

"No, I'm the guy responsible for getting you places on time and prepared."

"Have I ever been *un*prepared?" Darcy demanded.

"You're giving that speech at noon tomorrow," Bryan warned. "If it isn't finished you'd better get right on it. You don't want to show up looking dissipated from lack of sleep."

The harried parking attendant came over to Bryan. "Would you please move your car, sir?"

The dinner dance was breaking up and there were now a lot of people waiting for their cars to be brought around. Bryan's Toyota was blocking all the others.

"Sorry." He took Glory's arm again and hurried her toward the passenger side.

There was absolutely nothing she could do about it. Her eyes met Darcy's for one moment before Bryan opened the door, and Glory didn't know whether to laugh or cry. She only hoped her own emotions weren't as clearly evident.

"Darcy must have been tired tonight," Bryan re-

97

marked as they drove away. "He was downright testy just now. Did you notice? That isn't like him."

"Oh . . . well, you said yourself that it's been a long day."

"It never bothered him before. I've seen him party most of the night, grab a few hours of sleep, and beat the robins for sassiness the next morning. Of course I'll admit that that kind of athletics was some years ago."

"You knew him before the campaign?"

Bryan nodded. "He and my older brother went to law school together. They were a rare pair!" Admiration shone in his eyes. "When they wanted to get any studying done they used to have me take their calls. The phone never stopped ringing."

"It's remarkable that they ever graduated," Glory commented dryly.

"With honors," Bryan assured her.

"Do they still see each other?"

"They keep in touch, but Allen is married and has a couple of kids."

"It's surprising that Darcy hasn't been snapped up by now." Glory kept her voice carefully casual. "Hasn't he ever been serious about anyone?"

"There were a couple of girls, but nothing ever came of it."

"Nobody current?" Glory persisted.

"He was seeing a lady lawyer until recently, but come to think of it, I haven't heard him mention Linda's name lately. Probably because he's been too busy with the campaign. I imagine he'll get back to her. She's a real knockout."

"That's providing she's still waiting," Glory remarked distantly.

Bryan laughed. "I'd like to be as sure of everything in life."

Glory decided she'd heard enough about Darcy. She

98

changed the subject abruptly. "Tell me about your little girl. How old is Stephanie?"

"A remarkably mature four." Bryan chuckled. "She knows how to manipulate me expertly, something her mother didn't learn until she was twenty-two."

"You married very young, didn't you?"

"Yes, as soon as Joanie graduated from college. I had a good job by then, and there wasn't any reason to wait. We had three wonderful years together." He stared somberly at the road.

"I'm sorry, Bryan," Glory said contritely. "I shouldn't have brought it up."

"It's all right. I enjoy talking about Joanie."

"Would you like to tell me about her?" Glory asked softly.

Bryan was silent for a moment. Then he said, "She was beautiful. She had silky brown hair and big blue eyes, but the inner beauty that shone through was what made her special. Joanie had a heart as huge as she was tiny. She loved puppies and kittens—and babies." His voice flattened out.

"She sounds lovely," Glory commented when he seemed to be drifting toward painful remembrances.

"She wanted a baby so badly." Bryan might have been talking to himself. "After several miscarriages, I tried to convince her that she was enough for me, but Joanie wanted to try one last time." A muscle jerked in his tight jaw. "She died giving birth to Steffie."

"You mustn't blame yourself. I'm sure she knew the risks."

"Why did I let her take them?" He looked tortured. "I keep asking myself that question."

Glory put her hand on his arm. "Joanie wouldn't want you to. You can't live someone else's life for them, even out of love. She'd be happy that you have Steffie to help fill the void."

Mention of his daughter eased Bryan's tension, but he

still looked troubled. "She comes first with me, naturally, but I owe something to Darcy, too. It's a good thing I got there in time tonight. It would have been a serious mistake if he'd left early. Darcy ought to know that."

Glory felt guilty, realizing that Darcy did. He was a maverick, though. He was willing to give everything he had to the state senate except his personal life.

"I'd have been happy to baby-sit if you'd only asked me," she said. "Then you could have gone with him as you planned."

"That isn't part of your job," Bryan protested.

"I wouldn't have minded. I love children."

He grinned. "Don't make any rash offers. Reliable help is rarer than rubies."

Glory looked speculatively at Bryan's even features. He was really quite attractive. "Have you ever thought of getting married again? Not just for Steffie's sake," she said hurriedly. "I just meant that you're still so young."

His smile died. "I'd like to meet someone, but so far I haven't. No one would ever take Joanie's place, but I have a lot of love to give," he said simply.

Glory put her hand over his on the steering wheel. "You'll find someone, and she'll be a very lucky woman. You're a special person yourself, Bryan." So he wouldn't get the wrong idea, she added, "I'll be on the lookout for likely candidates."

"I'll trust your judgment. Just so long as she loves four-year-old girls and happens to be a raving beauty like you."

It was said jokingly. Glory realized that the chemistry wasn't there between Bryan and herself. They liked each other tremendously, but that's all there was. It would have been a lot easier if she'd been attracted to Bryan. He wasn't a bright elusive star like Darcy. But he didn't turn her bones to water either, with a single smiling glance.

As they pulled up in front of her house she said, "I'd love to meet Steffie. Perhaps you could bring her over some Saturday or Sunday. You might need me to baby-sit one day, and I wouldn't want to burst on her as a total stranger."

"That would be great! I hope it isn't an idle invitation because I'm apt to take you up on it."

"I hope you will," Glory told him.

As Bryan escorted her up the walk to her apartment he said, "You're a really super person. Darcy was lucky to find you."

"I was lucky to meet him, too," she answered soberly. "There aren't many men like him."

"That's sure true. He'd be a great state senator. We have an obligation to get him elected. The good he can do is worth any sacrifice." Bryan's smile lightened his serious expression. "Fortunately no one else is even within hollering distance."

"You really think it's in the bag?"

"Barring unforeseen errors, which Darcy is too smart to make." Bryan extended his hand. "You and I are bound for the big time, Ms. Prescott."

Bryan left, and Glory began getting undressed. She was filled with elation. Bryan was right. Darcy would win the election, and they would have the satisfaction of knowing they were partly responsible.

The telephone rang as she was getting into bed. Glory knew immediately who it was. She snuggled down under the covers and cradled the receiver against her cheek.

"I really can't believe this," Darcy groaned, without even saying hello. "Do you think it's a gigantic plot against us by the entire world?"

Glory laughed softly. His disappointment was very satisfying. "I don't think we should become paranoid. We just happen to be blessed with good friends who have our best interests at heart." It suddenly struck her

101

funny and she started to giggle. "They're obsessed with seeing that we get enough sleep."

"All I'm getting is cleaner. If I take one more cold shower, my skin is going to flake off! I had plans for us tonight, honey." As she clutched the phone tightly, Darcy's voice dropped another notch. "I could come over now."

She glanced at the clock, noticing how late it was. "Do you really have a speech to finish?"

He swore under his breath. "It won't take long. I can do it later."

With Bryan's pep talk ringing in her ears, Glory knew what she must do. It cost her a great deal, though. "You have to be prepared tomorrow. A lot of people are counting on you."

He sighed deeply. "I suppose you're right." There was a brief silence while they both regretted what might have been. "What are you doing?" Darcy asked abruptly.

"Nothing. I'm in bed."

"Oh, God!" he muttered. "Good night, Glory."

She hung up slowly, reluctant to break the tenuous contact. There was a smile on her face. Her earlier doubts were finally laid to rest. Darcy had meant it when he said she was special! A little thrill of excitement raced through Glory as she anticipated the following evening.

CHAPTER SIX

Darcy was in his office with Bryan and some other men when Glory got to work the next day. She hovered by the glass window for a few moments, wanting to say good morning, but he didn't glance over. Darcy's full attention was centered on the reports he was getting.

Glory went to her desk with a slightly let-down feeling, which she knew was foolish. She couldn't very well expect him to be waiting breathlessly for her to put in an appearance. With an unconscious sigh, she got out some folders and started to work.

Darcy's meeting lasted all morning. It was clearly an important one because Bryan transferred all their calls to Glory. Added to her other responsibilities, it made for a busy day, yet she still found time to glance over at Darcy's office. He didn't look her way even once.

Finally she went in to ask if the men wanted coffee. Although it wasn't one of her duties, Glory told herself it would be a thoughtful gesture.

Darcy was listening intently to one of the men. His slight frown turned into a smile when he saw her. It was a nice smile, but there was nothing special about it. "Good morning, Glory," he said pleasantly.

Bryan greeted her with a grin. "Hey, that's a good name. From now on I'm going to call you Morning Glory."

"I guess it's better than Petunia," she commented dryly. "Would anyone like coffee?"

Darcy answered for all of them. "Thanks, but we'll

be out of here in a few minutes." He glanced at his watch. "I have to get to that luncheon meeting."

They left a short time later. Glory looked up from her desk as they walked by, but Darcy was deep in conversation.

She watched them go with a feeling of annoyance. Darcy hadn't even told her what time he'd be back. What was she supposed to do about all the decisions that had to be made in his absence? In the back of her mind she realized he was paying her a compliment. Darcy trusted her to handle things. She was too hurt at his complete lack of interest to admit it, however. What had happened to the amorous man who was willing to stay up all night finishing a speech if it meant he could be with her for a few hours?

Glory was banging things around her desk when George came over. "What's the matter? Did someone tear down our posters?" he joked.

"No, I just remembered something Darcy said. He told me not to count my chickens before they were hatched." Her soft mouth set grimly. "I should have paid attention."

"Don't listen to him; he's too modest. We're halfway home. In a couple of months you'll be addressing him as Mr. Senator."

"Providing he talks to the common folk," she muttered.

"You know better than that, Glory. Darcy is the most down-to-earth guy you'll ever meet. Why else are all of us working our tail feathers off for him? I've been in politics a lot longer than you, and I've never met a man who inspired such loyalty. That's something you can't buy."

Glory knew everything George said was true. He made her ashamed of her grumbling. It was stupid to resent the fact that Darcy hadn't given her a minute of his time. The strategy meeting was obviously important.

The sparkle returned to her eyes as she thought ahead to that evening. They hadn't had a chance to make plans, but after Darcy's frustration the previous night, it was almost a foregone conclusion that he expected to see her.

It was late afternoon before Darcy and Bryan got back to the office. Then there were phone calls to be returned and other business to take care of. It wasn't until an hour later that Darcy came out to the big room that housed all their desks. His tie was loosened and his rolled-up sleeves exposed tanned forearms with a sprinkling of dark hair.

From under her lowered lashes Glory watched the coordinated way his lithe body moved. Darcy was the eye of the storm. He was completely relaxed, but he charged the air around him. The atmosphere picked up excitement when he entered a room.

After getting himself some coffee, he came over to settle one hip on the edge of Glory's desk. He smiled, and this time there were tiny lights in his eyes—restrained but definitely there. "How was your day?" he asked.

"Hectic," she answered. "How was yours?"

"The same. Bryan has me on such a tight schedule that I think there's a time limit on brushing my teeth."

"You have to give up the unimportant things to gain the important ones," she commented lightly.

"There are some things I'm not willing to give up," he said in a low voice.

Glory tried to suppress the surge of pleasure she felt. "Don't tell Bryan that."

"He's only in charge of my professional life." Darcy's eyes glinted mischievously. "Although, I must admit he's done a good job of hashing up my private one."

"I guess he doesn't think a candidate has a right to one. Poor Bryan, he doesn't have much of a personal life himself. He was telling me about his wife last night."

Darcy's face sobered. "She was a lovely woman. I don't think he'll ever get over losing her."

"Isn't he seeing anyone? It's been more than four years."

Darcy shook his head. "He doesn't have time actually. Bryan feels he should have dinner with Steffie when he isn't working, and every weekend is devoted to her. It doesn't leave much room for dating. I can understand it, though. The poor little kid is with strangers all day long."

Glory nodded. "He's trying to be both father and mother to her, and that's tough."

Darcy sighed. "I wish he could meet a nice girl and get married, but it would take a special kind of woman."

Mitchell joined them, wearing a worried expression. "Can I talk to you when you have a minute, chief? I think we have a conflict on two speaking dates."

"Sure. What's the problem?" Darcy walked with the other man over to his desk.

Glory watched them go with a feeling of frustration. It was the first moment she'd had with Darcy all day! It also bothered Glory that he hadn't asked to see her that evening, but she comforted herself with the thought that he hadn't had the chance.

After he resolved Mitchell's problem, Darcy went back into his own office. As it grew later, one person after another drifted out. Even Bryan called it a day.

He stopped at Glory's desk. "It's quitting time, in case you hadn't noticed."

"I just have a deposit to make up for tomorrow morning. The way contributions are coming in you'd think Darcy invented a diet that included a hot fudge sundae every day."

"Why didn't I think of that!" Bryan exclaimed.

Glory laughed. "Because all the people who gained fifteen pounds by election time would vote against him."

"I knew there had to be a reason." Bryan chuckled and reached in his pocket for his car keys. "Come on, I'll give you a ride home."

"Oh—uh—well, I have something to do first. You go ahead, Bryan."

"I'd wait for you, but I told Steffie I'd be home early tonight," he said apologetically. "It's one of our rare free nights."

"I understand perfectly," Glory assured him. He couldn't have given her better news.

The office took on an unaccustomed quiet after Bryan left. There were only Darcy and herself remaining. Through the glass window, she saw him hang up the phone. Glory went into his office and stood in the doorway. "Bryan says it's time to go home."

Darcy's face lighted with laughter. "That's tantamount to a ruling by the Supreme Court."

"That's what I thought."

An undercurrent of awareness passed between them as they stared at each other. Before Darcy could answer, the phone rang. He made a face as he picked up the receiver.

His expression changed when he recognized the caller. "How nice to hear from you, Marsha." He listened for a brief moment before saying, "Well, that sounds very promising, but—" The woman interrupted with what must have been a compelling argument. Darcy glanced irresolutely at Glory. "I understand what you're saying . . . Yes, I realize we might not have another opportunity like this for weeks . . . I know what trouble it was to set this up, and I don't like to disappoint you."

Glory's slight figure stiffened. Her first impulse when she heard Darcy talking to another woman had been to leave him alone. Now she was glad she hadn't. His indecision expressed volumes. Marsha, whoever she was, had clearly moved heaven and earth to spend an evening with Darcy. It didn't console Glory one bit that he was torn between the two of them. Marsha could have him!

She turned abruptly. "Good night, Darcy."

"Glory, wait!"

"I'm late for a date," she lied, making a hasty exit.

Depression accompanied her to the bus and all the way home. It was time to get off the roller coaster. She had spent half her time the last two days on top of a mountain, and the other half down in the pits. One minute she was sure Darcy cared about her, the next she was sure he didn't. Tonight was the last straw!

She knew his neglect all day could be explained away, but not his conduct tonight. If he had really meant all the sweet talk he buttered her up with, Darcy would have told that other woman immediately that he was busy. But he wanted to keep all his options open. Their tentative relationship had been plagued with obstacles. Perhaps he wanted to go with a sure thing, Glory thought bitterly.

Her soft mouth drooped and her brows were drawn together in a frown as she got out her key. When the lock stuck she kicked the door in an excess of frustration.

Ellen opened her own door at the repeated banging. "Problems?"

"That's putting it mildly," Glory muttered.

"Sometimes you have to lift up on the knob while you turn the key." Ellen grinned. "These doors are older than we are. They need tender loving care."

Glory scowled. "None of the rest of us get it . . . Why should they?"

Ellen raised her eyebrows. "My goodness, we are in a stew, aren't we?"

"As Queen Victoria said, *we* are not amused," Glory remarked coldly.

"Sorry," Ellen murmured. "I guess my timing was off."

Glory sighed. "No, *I'm* sorry. I had a rotten day."

"So did I. Why don't we compare notes?" Ellen beckoned Glory in and led the way to the kitchen. She took a bottle of wine out of the refrigerator. "I think the occasion calls for more than iced tea." When they had taken their glasses into the living room, Ellen said, "Do you want to go first, or should I?"

Glory stared moodily into her white wine. "There isn't anything to tell. It was just one of those days."

"Uh-huh," Ellen said skeptically. "You always come home and kick the door when the bus is late. What's the matter—did Mr. Wonderful slip in the polls?"

"No, I imagine he'll be elected by a landslide," Glory replied distantly.

"You sound as happy as if you were working for his opponent," Ellen remarked dryly.

"I don't know where you get that impression. I couldn't be more delighted."

"You could have fooled me. What's wrong, Glory?"

"Nothing," she insisted.

Glory knew that Ellen was bound to say I told you so if she related the events of last night and today. And that was the last thing she wanted to hear. It was bad enough to have made a fool of herself. At least no one else knew about her expectations.

"What ruined *your* day?" she asked Ellen to distract her.

"The same thing that always does—a man."

"Well, I'll say one thing for you, you're consistent." Glory frowned. "Can't we talk about something else?"

"I'd be glad to, but that seems to be what's on your mind." Ellen's generous mouth thinned in disapproval. "When are you going to stop letting that handsome hulk pull your strings like a puppeteer? He either has you dancing for joy or collapsed in a pool of misery."

"No man has the power to make me miserable anymore," Glory stated firmly.

"That's the right spirit. Now all you have to do is mean it."

"How can I convince you?"

"Act a little happier about it. What did the guy do to you?"

"Nothing," Glory said flatly. She pushed the long hair back from her delicate face. When Ellen just waited, she added reluctantly, "I honestly thought Darcy was different."

"That was your *first* mistake."

"Well, he did help me find this apartment, and he gave me a job."

"All so he could make a move when the time was ripe," Ellen snorted. "You had a date with him last night, didn't you? What did he do today, say thanks for the memories, but I don't think we should get serious?"

"No, you don't understand! We didn't—" Glory broke off, her face reddening.

"Oh, I see." Ellen nodded her head knowingly. "He was in a snit because you wouldn't."

"It isn't like that at all." Glory sighed. "I may as well tell you. I thought Darcy was interested in me, but now I don't think he is."

"That's not the impression I got when he was making himself a fixture around here."

"I thought that, too, but we were both wrong. Oh, sure, I guess he wouldn't mind a quick fling." Glory carefully picked a piece of lint off her skirt. "Darcy is a very virile man. I suppose that's what confused me. I thought there was more to it than sex."

"What made you change your mind?"

"We were about to make plans for tonight when a

110

woman called him. I presume she made him a better offer," Glory said bitterly.

"The rat!"

Glory tried to smile. "It didn't exactly make my Friday night."

"You're lucky to have found out before you got involved," Ellen assured her. "Those handsome ones are the worst. They're spoiled rotten because they have so many panting women to choose from."

"It's positively disgusting the way they were throwing themselves at him last night!" Glory exclaimed angrily. "You'd think women would have more pride. They could at least wait until they were asked!"

Ellen grinned. *"You* did, and someone walked off with your lollipop."

"Whose side are you on, anyway?"

"Yours. I was just pointing out the obvious. Also, the bigger the fish, the harder it is to land him." Ellen shrugged. "Personally, I never saw one that was worth the effort. Men and fish are a lot alike. They go bad after a couple of days."

Glory smiled unwillingly. "I thought that was house-guests."

"Same category—they're both to be avoided like the plague. Take my advice and tell him to get lost when he turns those big topaz eyes on you and tries to apologize."

"Good thinking," Glory replied more positively than she felt.

It was revealing that Ellen, the man hater, had noticed the unusual color of Darcy's eyes. She hadn't seen them with that special glow, though. Could even Ellen have resisted him? Glory experienced an aching sense of loss.

"If you feel you absolutely have to fall in love, at least pick a nice ordinary guy," Ellen advised. "Not a superstar."

"He is special, isn't he?" Glory asked softly.

"That's what they call the daily blue plate at our cafeteria: the special. It still gives everybody indigestion." The phone rang before Glory could answer. Ellen's grim expression lightened at the caller's voice. "Hi, Mrs. Belmont. What's up?"

"My dear, I got simply carried away this afternoon," the older woman said. "I made so much coq au vin that I'll have to eat it for days if you don't come up and help me."

"Well, I don't know," Ellen hesitated. "Glory is here and we—"

"Splendid!" Mrs. Belmont interrupted. "I intended to call her, too. Do come along, both of you."

Ellen put her hand over the phone. "It's Mrs. Belmont. Do you want to drown your sorrows in chicken and wine sauce?"

Glory held up her glass. "Sure. Why not? We already have a head start." As they carried the glasses out to the kitchen she commented, "You spend a lot of time with her, don't you?"

"She's really a darling," Ellen replied. "Sometimes I'd honestly rather be alone, but I know she's lonely, so I rarely turn her down."

"You're truly a very nice person."

Ellen raised an eyebrow. "Don't sound so surprised. I'm kind to animals, too, and I don't make children cry."

"You just stick pins in little male dolls," Glory teased.

Ellen grinned. "Everybody's entitled to a hobby."

As they were going up the stairs Glory's phone started ringing. "Let it ring," she said curtly.

"That's the old fight." Ellen laughed. "There might be hope for you yet."

Mrs. Belmont had set the table with her best china

and silver. She was wearing a long hostess gown, and her small withered face was wreathed in smiles.

"Isn't this lovely?" she beamed. "We're going to have a hen party, if you'll excuse the pun. It's just too bad that Darcy isn't here to join us, though. I did so enjoy talking to him the other evening."

"You enjoy talking to everyone," Ellen teased.

The old lady smiled mischievously. "Especially those who haven't already heard my stories, you mean?"

Ellen's warm regard was full of affection. "I have no complaints."

"You're very kind, my dear. However, I must admit that it's nice to have a little male attention. One of these nights I plan to give a real dinner party. Perhaps Darcy might bring a young man for you."

"Oh, goody," Ellen murmured sarcastically.

Glory hurriedly changed the subject. "The table looks beautiful. Where did you find those stunning place mats? I'd love to get some."

"Ellen brought them to me," Mrs. Belmont answered.

"They came from Bryman's," Ellen remarked. "They have quite a good selection. If you pick out what you want, I'll get you my employee's discount."

"Great! I'll take you up on it," Glory said.

"I have to work a half day tomorrow, but I could meet you at one," Ellen offered.

"It's a date. Would you like to join us, Mrs. Belmont?" Glory asked.

"Thank you, dear, but I have a man coming to give me an estimate on painting my apartment. Do you think I should stick with cream-colored walls or do something really daring?"

The old lady was successfully diverted onto the subject of decorating—and away from Darcy. To Glory's relief, his name wasn't mentioned again all evening.

* * *

Glory was up early the next morning. She was dusting her apartment when the phone rang. For a moment she was tempted to ignore it, but she realized that was silly. She couldn't avoid Darcy forever.

If he tried to apologize, she would assure him coolly that no apologies were necessary. She'd tell him that it was all in his own mind because she had been invited to a dinner party the previous night. If he thought she was home waiting by the phone, he was very badly mistaken, although of course she wouldn't tell him *that*. She'd treat the whole matter of his defection as supremely unimportant.

When it wasn't Darcy on the phone, Glory was furious.

"I hope this isn't too early for you," Bryan said tentatively.

"Not at all," Glory answered, stifling her anger with difficulty. "Did something unexpected come up?"

"No, don't worry. I didn't call to ruin your Saturday. Steffie and I are going to the park today, and I thought if you really meant it about getting to know her . . ." His voice trailed off uncertainly. "You probably have plans, though."

"Not until one o'clock. If you're going this morning, I'd love to join you."

"That would be great! I'll make some sandwiches and we'll have a picnic," Bryan said. "Mrs. Maxwell is off on the weekends, and we fend for ourselves."

"Let me make the sandwiches," Glory offered.

"I don't want you to go to any trouble. That wasn't why I asked you."

"I know, and it isn't any trouble. Just give me half an hour."

Glory changed from her jeans to a pair of white linen pants. A voluminous dark green shirt went over them, cinched by a white belt with a silver buckle. It was a

114

casual outfit, but she managed to look exceedingly feminine. Her flame red hair tumbling around her shoulders
was an attention getter, along with her tiny waist and
long slim legs.

The sandwiches and a sack of potato chips went into
a large paper bag. Glory was just adding a package of
chocolate chip cookies when the doorbell rang.

"That was good timing," she remarked as she opened
the door. "I'm all ready."

The little girl looked tiny standing next to her father.
Her silky light brown hair was pulled back in a
ponytail, and her wide blue eyes gazed up at Glory with
interest.

"This is Steffie," Bryan said with quiet pride.

"It's so nice to meet you, Steffie," Glory said. "I hope
we're going to be good friends."

"I don't have any grown-up friends," the little girl
replied doubtfully. "Do you know how to play hopscotch?"

"I was kindergarten champion," Glory declared sol-
emnly.

"Will you play with me?" Steffie asked eagerly.

"You bet! Anytime you say."

Glory handed the bag of lunch to Bryan and locked
her door. When they started down the hall, Stephanie
took her hand, chattering about plans for the day. Her
small face was filled with animation.

"You made an instant hit," Bryan murmured in
Glory's ear.

"She's adorable," Glory answered warmly. The little
girl was so open and friendly that she'd win anyone's
heart.

Mrs. Belmont was watering the row of bright gerani-
ums that lined the walk. Her hair was still arranged in
its intricate hairdo from the night before, including the
long jeweled pins that secured her chignon. But she was
wearing an army surplus flight jacket over one of her

115

many pairs of vivid polyester slacks—canary yellow this time.

Glory smothered a grin at Bryan's expression. Mrs. Belmont had that effect on people seeing her for the first time.

"Where are you off to so early in the morning?" The old lady's interested gaze swept over Bryan and his daughter as Glory introduced them.

"We're going to have a picnic in the park," Steffie announced. "Do you want to come?" Without waiting for an answer she tugged at Glory's hand. "Does she know how to play hopscotch?"

Glory smiled. "It wouldn't surprise me."

The old lady said, "Thank you for the nice invitation, missy, but I have to finish my gardening. You be sure to have a good time."

"She's . . . uh . . . rather unusual, isn't she?" Bryan asked as they pulled away from the curb in his Toyota.

Glory laughed. "That's what I thought when I first met her. Darcy was the one who told me not to be fooled by appearances."

"Darcy's met her?"

Glory's lips twitched at the memory of her ill-fated dinner party. "He spent an evening with her. Mrs. Belmont adored him."

"I told you Darcy scored with women from eight to eighty." Bryan grinned.

Glory's smiled faded. "Yes, I believe you mentioned it."

The first thing they did when they got to the park was ride in one of the little boats on the lake, at Steffie's request. Glory was very impressed with the way Bryan handled his daughter. Although he obviously adored her and allowed her a great deal of leeway, he could be quietly firm. When he said no, she didn't argue or sulk.

Glory commented on it to Bryan while she was putting out lunch on the blanket he'd brought. Steffie was at the water's edge, feeding the ducks with crumbs of bread.

"She's the most unspoiled child I've ever met," Glory told him.

"How many do you know?" he replied, chuckling.

"Enough to know you've done a fantastic job. It would be so easy to overindulge her. I think it's amazing that you haven't."

Steffie came running back before he could acknowledge the compliment. "All my bread is gone. Can I have some more?" she asked.

"It's time for lunch now. We'll save some of the crusts," Glory promised.

She was packing up the debris after they'd eaten when the little girl sprang to her feet. "It's Uncle Darcy! Look, Daddy, it's Uncle Darcy!"

Glory's breathing quickened as she glanced up and saw him strolling toward them. Darcy looked potently masculine in tight jeans that rode low on his narrow hips. His hands were thrust in the pockets, tightening the fabric over his long muscular thighs. A plaid shirt was open at the throat, revealing dark curling hair.

"Hey, this is a surprise!" Bryan's delight matched his daughter's. "What are you doing here?"

"I stopped by Glory's and Mrs. Belmont told me where you were, so I thought I'd drop by." Darcy's enigmatic gaze rested on Glory. He was aware, even if Bryan wasn't, that she hadn't added her greetings to the others'.

"Too bad you didn't get here a few minutes sooner," Bryan said. "We just finished lunch. Is there anything left, Glory?"

"Just a few cookies." She stood up. "I'll leave you to get rid of the trash."

Darcy frowned. "I didn't mean to scare you away."

117

"You didn't," she answered coolly. "I have an appointment downtown."

"I'll drive you."

"No, thanks. I'll take the bus."

"I said I'd drive you." His fingers curled firmly around her upper arm.

Since it was a question of making a scene or going with him, Glory didn't have much choice. When they were out of earshot she said angrily, "I don't know why you were so insistent."

"I want to talk to you."

"We have nothing to talk about," she muttered.

"I think we have a great deal."

Glory glanced at him out of the corner of her eye. The square line of his jaw was taut. Darcy didn't look like a man about to apologize, but what else could he have to say to her? She resolved that if he did try to make amends for his behavior the night before, she would remember Ellen's advice. Glory's small chin set as grimly as his. Those sexy topaz eyes weren't going to have any effect this time!

CHAPTER SEVEN

After helping Glory into the sporty silver Mercedes, Darcy got in on the driver's side. But he didn't turn on the motor.

"All right, suppose you tell me what's wrong," he said quietly.

"I have no idea what you're talking about." She stared straight ahead. "Can we get started? I have a one o'clock appointment and I don't want to be late."

"I'll get you there in plenty of time. First, I want to know why you went flying out of my office in such a snit last night?"

"I wasn't in a snit. It was quitting time."

"Since when have you become a clock-watcher?"

She turned to face him indignantly. "All the others were gone! Why did you expect *me* to stay on?"

His slow smile raised little goose bumps. "That's a foolish question."

Glory ignored the warmth creeping over her. "If you're not satisfied with my work, why don't you come out and say so?"

"I'm a long way from satisfied, but it has nothing to do with your work." Darcy took hold of her hand and held on when she would have pulled it away. His thumb massaged the soft skin of her wrist maddeningly. "It was the first minute we'd had alone all day."

"Just the two of us and Marsha!" The words burst out in spite of Glory's resolve.

"Is *that* what bothered you?" he exclaimed incredulously.

"Not at all. What difference does it make to me who you spend your time with?"

"Marsha is the wife of one of my biggest backers," Darcy explained patiently. "I couldn't turn her down."

"That's disgusting!" Glory succeeded in jerking her hand away. "What happened to all those high-flown principles you're always talking about?"

Darcy frowned. "What are *you* talking about? She called to tell me that Dennis, her husband, had gotten together five of the most influential businessmen in town. It was a last-minute thing because they all have so many commitments. Dennis wanted me to meet with them at a small intimate gathering. He was confident that they'd back my candidacy if they liked what I had to say. What principles did I compromise? It was just a straightforward clarification of some questions they raised."

Glory couldn't look at him. Had she really jumped to conclusions too quickly? Knowing Darcy as she did, how could she have doubted him?

He jerked her chin up. "If you were thinking what it sounds like, I ought to turn you over my knee and whack some sense into at least one end of you!" His wide mouth was compressed in anger.

"I'm sorry, Darcy. Truly I am."

"You admit it, then?" he demanded.

"Well, it just sounded . . . I mean, you were so interested all of a sudden. I couldn't help . . ." She stumbled to a halt.

"I would have given *you* the benefit of the doubt," he said sternly.

Glory's head drooped. "You're a nicer person than I am."

"Evidently." His tone was inflexible, but there was a smile in his eyes that she didn't see.

"I wouldn't blame you if you never forgave me."

"Well, that's a little harsh. Are you willing to make amends?"

"I'll do anything!" she breathed.

Darcy's smile was broad now. "As a lawyer, I'd caution you against such a sweeping promise."

Glory returned his smile tremulously. "I know you wouldn't take advantage of it."

"Don't be so trusting." His hands were on her shoulders, drawing her slowly toward him. "Let's go to my place and see how much willpower I have."

Glory had to use all her own willpower to keep from throwing her arms around his neck. She wanted to curl up in his lap and slide her lips up the firm column of his neck until they reached his irresistible mouth.

"Does that appeal to you, my love?" He tangled his fingers in her hair and pulled her head back gently.

As she was about to agree eagerly she remembered her date with Ellen. "I can't," she groaned. "I have an appointment at one."

"Can't you call and change it?" Darcy coaxed as he stroked the soft skin in back of her ear.

"I'm meeting a friend in the linen department at Bryman's. There's no way I can get in touch with her now, and I can't just leave her standing there."

He sighed. "I suppose not."

As they stared impotently at each other Glory murmured, "I'm free tonight."

Darcy closed his eyes briefly. "I have to drive to Santa Barbara late this afternoon to appear at a benefit. These few hours are all I have today."

"I could drive up with you," she offered tentatively.

"Dennis Hadley is going along," Darcy said reluctantly.

Glory tried to laugh, because the alternative was crying. "I guess it just wasn't meant to be."

"Don't say that!" Darcy gathered her fiercely in his

arms, burying his face in her bright hair. "When I come back we're going to make some time for ourselves, no matter who we have to disappoint!"

His tight embrace was so satisfying that Glory had to force herself to draw away. "Someone might see us."

"I don't care! This is a pale imitation of what I'd like to be doing." His mouth trailed a burning path down her cheek. "I want to make love to you slowly—with all the time in the world. I want to kiss every secret place on your beautiful body until you need me as much as I need you. And then I—"

Glory put trembling fingers over his mouth. "Don't, Darcy!" she pleaded.

He kissed her fingertips. "You're right, angel. I'm just making it harder for both of us." He took a deep breath before releasing her and starting the motor. "We have a date when I come back, and I don't intend to let anyone or anything stand in the way." Darcy's strong face expressed grim determination. "Is that clear?"

The happiness that filled Glory almost compensated for the unfulfilled ache. She gave a breathy little laugh. "I wouldn't dream of disagreeing with you, chief."

Ellen was waiting impatiently when Glory hurried into the linen department. "I was beginning to wonder what happened to you," she said.

"I'm sorry. I . . . I had a rather hectic morning."

Ellen looked more closely at her friend's flushed cheeks and barely suppressed excitement. "So it would seem. What's going on?"

Glory didn't want to tell her about Darcy, knowing how she would react. Ellen was wrong, but there was no convincing her, so Glory settled for part of the story. "Bryan Trent called this morning. Remember, I told you about him? He's the one with the little girl. She's an adorable child—so outgoing for a four-year-old. I fell in love with her." The words came out in a rush.

Ellen looked at her speculatively. "All this enthusiasm over a child seems a trifle much. It couldn't be the father you're interested in, could it?"

"Don't be ridiculous! Bryan's a darling, but he's just a friend."

"Uh-huh. A friend who's so fascinating he made you forget what time it was? Did it ever occur to you that you might be rebounding like a rubber ball?"

"You're way off base! I told Bryan I'd like to meet his daughter sometime, so he called and said they were going to the park and asked if I would like to join them. That's all there was to it. We rode in one of the little boats and ate tuna fish sandwiches."

Ellen's eyes narrowed suspiciously. "Didn't you say Bryan is Darcy's campaign manager? Mr. Rich and Famous didn't happen to be along on this picnic, did he?"

"No, he got there after—" Glory stopped abruptly.

"I thought so!"

"You're wrong, Ellen. Darcy isn't—" She paused as they were jostled by shoppers. "Let's go have coffee someplace where we can talk."

When they were seated at one of the tables in the store cafeteria, Glory said quietly, "We were both wrong about Darcy, but I was guiltier because I know him and you don't." She told Ellen the whole story of her misconception the night before. "It's been that way every time I had doubts about him. I made my own troubles. In a way, I was like you—I couldn't believe there could be a man who was absolutely straightforward. I know now that Darcy is that man."

"He's interested in your quick mind," Ellen remarked mockingly.

"I hope so, but he's also very honest about wanting to make love to me. How can I be indignant when that's what I want, too? The chemistry between us is awesome."

Ellen looked troubled. "He's a very dynamic man—

it's understandable. I'm just worried that it's more than a physical attraction for you."

"It is. I'm in love with him," Glory answered softly, admitting what she could no longer deny. Darcy filled her whole world. He was the man she wanted to spend the rest of her life with.

"Does he love you?" Ellen asked somberly.

"I don't know, but it doesn't change anything. You can't turn love on or off because it's sensible."

"You could get hurt badly."

Glory's eyes darkened to jade. "I can also store up memories that other women are never fortunate enough to have. A short time with Darcy will be more exciting than a lifetime with anyone else."

Ellen sighed heavily. "I hope you know what you're doing."

"I don't have any choice," Glory answered simply.

Glory was trying to read that night. Unfortunately she had chosen a romantic novel, and every love scene reminded her of Darcy. When he called, it was like an answer to her prayers, but his voice was grim.

"You won't believe it, sweetheart, but I have to stay over tomorrow."

"Oh, Darcy, no!"

"That's what *I* said, but it didn't get me very far. Dennis set up a fishing trip on some tycoon's yacht. As I understand it, the object is to pour just enough drinks into the assembled V.I.P.'s to make them mellow but not too befuddled to sign checks."

"I hope they all get seasick!"

"Don't say that. Then the whole trip would be a waste."

"That's true." Glory tried to force down her disappointment. "It's too bad the best man can't win on his merits, but money *is* indispensable for winning an election."

"I'm beginning to have my doubts about politics," Darcy said sullenly. "Maybe I'm not cut out for it. I got into this thing because I honestly thought I could do some good, but for two cents, I'd chuck the whole enchilada!"

"You don't mean that," Glory told him. "I know it goes against the grain, but it will all be worth it."

"Not if it keeps us apart," he said adamantly. "You've become very important to me, Glory."

His words were more precious than a gift of jewels. "Sunday is always followed by Monday," she said softly.

"And Monday night," he added throatily. "Is it a date?"

"As far as I'm concerned." She laughed. "I don't have the commitments you do."

"You're my commitment." His voice had a deep masculine sound. "Get a lot of sleep this weekend, angel. You're going to need it."

Glory could hardly wait for Monday morning to arrive. On the way to work she couldn't help worrying that something might have happened to delay Darcy again, but her fears were unfounded. He was already at his desk. He looked up and smiled at her through the glass partition, a smile full of meaning.

Glory didn't intend to stand on ceremony this time, but before she could go into Darcy's office, her phone rang. Sally hovered impatiently, waiting to talk to her, and the others all had something that also needed her attention. Just as the last one went out the door, Bryan took a sheaf of papers into the inner office. Glory sighed and began to open the mail as she waited for a moment alone with Darcy.

His angry voice was so unexpected that it startled her. Darcy never lost his temper. He was always an oasis of calm when the rest of them got excited. Something really horrendous must have happened. Through the glass window, Glory could see that his entire body was taut.

Although the door was closed, Darcy's words were loud enough to be heard. *"I won't do it!"*

Bryan's softer response wasn't audible.

"There's simply no end to these things, and I'm sick of it!" Darcy glared at his manager. "I happen to be a man, not a machine!"

When Bryan didn't seem able to placate him, Glory went into Darcy's office. "I don't know what's going on, but they can hear you all the way to the bus stop. What's the trouble?"

Darcy looked broodingly at her. "Bryan has just informed me that I'm addressing a meeting of the Bar Association tonight."

"Oh." They stared at each other wordlessly.

"It's been on your calendar for weeks. You just forgot about it." Bryan tried to lighten the atmosphere with a weak joke. "If you don't show up, these guys might sue you just for practice."

"If Glory will step out of the room for a moment, I'll tell you what else they can do," Darcy said grimly.

"Maybe you can talk some sense into him." Bryan turned helplessly to Glory.

She was caught between the bark and the tree. Glory was every bit as disappinted as Darcy, but if she didn't side with Bryan, Darcy stood to lose a lot of credibility.

"You really have to go, Darcy." She attempted a smile. "Maybe it will be an early evening."

Bryan looked troubled. "There's no point in holding out false hopes. Darcy is the last speaker, and then there's a question-and-answer period."

Darcy swore savagely under his breath before heading for the door. "I'm going to get some coffee."

The air still seemed to vibrate after he had gone.

Bryan whistled. "I've never seen him like this. I don't know what's gotten into him."

"You *have* been keeping him on an awfully tight schedule," Glory pointed out.

"He never minded before. Darcy thrives on hard work."

"Even Superman changes out of his cape now and then. What's the rest of his week like?" Glory asked innocently.

Bryan's expression was worried. "With the mood he's in right now, I'm afraid to tell him."

She sighed. "That bad?"

"It's the weekend I'm worried about. I want to talk to you about that, too, Glory. We got an invitation from some San Francisco bigwigs. Most of them have summer homes in Lake Tahoe, where I understand they party every weekend."

"Darcy will go into orbit if you suggest he give up his small amount of free time for a social event!" Glory exclaimed.

"You know I wouldn't do that. They're having a candidate's day this weekend, and I think he should be there. Darcy really needs exposure up north. He's a household word down here, but those people don't know enough about him. They're worried about all kinds of things—diverting the rivers, uneven distribution of taxes, a whole Pandora's box that Darcy can put a lid on."

"You really think that a social gathering is the right forum?"

"The event doesn't matter; it's the people he can reach. They're the opinion makers."

Glory sighed again as she saw another week slip by. "I suppose you're right."

"I know I am. What I wanted to ask is, Will you go with Darcy? I know it's an imposition," he said hurriedly as she stared at him in amazement, "but I really hate to leave Steffie alone on the weekends. Mrs. Maxwell won't stay, so it means getting someone from an agency. I'd really appreciate it, Glory," he coaxed. "Will you do it?"

She tried to keep the excitement out of her voice. A whole weekend alone with Darcy! Well, almost alone. "I'd be happy to, Bryan. I'll even convince him to go—no matter how difficult it is," Glory said, trying to keep a deadpan expression on her face.

"That would be great!" Bryan glanced apprehensively through the glass pane. "Fasten your seat belt. Here he comes, and he looks like a bear with an ingrown toenail."

"Leave me alone with him," she advised.

"I won't forget this," Bryan murmured hurriedly.

Glory smiled bewitchingly. "I won't either."

Darcy had gotten his temper under control, but he still looked dangerously forbidding. "I'm sorry," he said austerely. They were both included in the apology, although his gaze lingered on Glory. "I'm afraid I overreacted."

"That's okay, chief. I understand," Bryan said soothingly. "It will all be worth it, though. You'll see."

"I'll take your word for it." Darcy looked broodingly at Glory.

"I have to get to the bank," Bryan said hastily.

There was silence in the inner office until he went out the front door. Then Darcy turned to Glory. "What can I say? My life isn't my own anymore."

"It will be. You were very hard on Bryan just now. He's only doing his job."

"I know that." Darcy jammed his hands in his pockets. "I behaved abominably."

Glory laughed. "Well, your halo did tilt a bit, but I imagine he'll forgive you."

"Will you, Glory? I keep breaking one date after another with you."

"It doesn't matter," she assured him.

"It does to me. You don't know how much I was looking forward to this evening. Not just to make love to you." Darcy lifted her chin in his palm and looked compellingly into her eyes. "I enjoy being with you. I like sitting across a dinner table and talking to you. I want to walk on the beach hand in hand, go to the movies . . . I want to *be* with you."

Glory had a lump in her throat. "I think that's the nicest compliment a man has ever paid me."

"I want to be the man in your life, sweetheart, but how long can I ask you to wait when I can't even give you one evening?"

"We'll have one," she said softly.

"When?" He groaned. "Bryan probably has me booked every night this week."

"He does, including next weekend." As Darcy's face started to darken she added, "But it might not be so bad. He thinks you should attend a bipartisan party at Lake Tahoe. It's a vacation spot."

"For everyone except me!" Darcy bit out grimly.

Glory smiled enchantingly. "Oh, I don't know. We might manage a little free time."

He looked at her uncertainly. "We?"

"Bryan asked me, as a great favor, if I'd go with you in his place." Her eyes sparkled with laughter. "I told him I'd make the sacrifice."

A slow smile smoothed the harsh lines from Darcy's face. He touched her cheek gently. "I'll try to make it as easy for you as possible."

That week was especially busy as the campaign heated up. The only personal contact they had was on the phone at night. Darcy called when he got home from whatever function he'd attended, and they talked until Glory made him go to bed. It would have been frustrating if they hadn't had something to look forward to.

One day toward the end of the week, Bryan stopped by Glory's desk. "I've got to hand it to you, Morning Glory. Ever since you calmed Darcy down on Black Monday, he's been his old self again. What did you say to him?"

"I can't take the credit," she answered demurely. "Darcy realizes he has obligations. They just overwhelmed him for a few minutes."

"I can relate to that," Bryan remarked somberly. "I don't know what I'm going to do about Steffie. For the first time in her life she's acting up."

"That's hard to believe! She was so adorable the other day. What's the problem?"

"I guess she's feeling neglected. I can't seem to manage much time with her lately. I used to sit with her during dinner even if I couldn't eat with her, but I haven't been home all week." He sighed heavily. "I don't see what I can do about it until Saturday either."

"Why don't you bring her over to my house for dinner tomorrow night?" Glory suggested. "She knows me now, and it'll make her feel important to have someplace to go like a grown-up."

"Would you really do that?" Bryan looked almost pathetically grateful. "I hate to ask you to give up an evening, but it would make all the difference in the world. I know she's feeling unloved at the moment."

Glory smiled wryly. "I've kicked a few doors myself when I was feeling that way. Believe me, it's no fun! Bring Steffie to me and I'll see what I can do about cheering her up. She can even stay overnight if it would be easier for you."

"Thanks, but she has to go to nursery school in the morning, so I'd better pick her up on my way home."

"Won't that be past her bedtime?"

"I'll bring her nightgown, and you can put her to

130

sleep in your bed. She won't wake when I carry her out to the car."

"Okay, whatever you think best."

"You're a living doll, Glory! This is two I owe you—first Darcy and now Steffie. Maybe I can solve some problems for you one day."

Glory smiled as she turned to answer the phone. Bryan didn't know it, but they were more than even.

Glory did her marketing on the way home from work the next day. She was juggling a large paper bag while trying to fit her key in the lock when Ellen came into the entrance hall.

"Need some help?" She took the bag from Glory. A large package of chocolate marshmallow cookies was poking out the top. "Do you know how fattening those things are? I'm gaining weight just holding them."

"You're okay if the cellophane wrapping isn't broken. And then it's still safe if you don't inhale." Glory got the door open and reclaimed her groceries. "Do you want to come for dinner tonight? I'm having Bryan's little girl, Steffie."

Ellen's eyebrows climbed. "Switching your affections so soon?"

"It's nothing like that." Glory carried her groceries into the kitchen with Ellen trailing after her. "Bryan has to work tonight, so I offered to make dinner for Steffie."

Ellen's expression changed to disgust. "Now they have you baby-sitting! You let everyone take advantage of you."

"If you knew Bryan, you'd realize how wrong you are. I offered."

"Uh-huh," Ellen said skeptically. "After he didn't leave you any way to refuse."

Glory glanced at the kitchen clock. "They'll be here

131

shortly. See if you don't change your mind after you meet him."

"No, thanks. I'm leaving. I've had my quota of thrills for today." Ellen grinned as she waved and left.

Glory sighed. Ellen was such a super person except for that one blind spot. But she didn't have time to worry about her neighbor just then. There was dinner to prepare and the table to set.

If Steffie had been obstreperous at home, there was no sign of it that evening. She chattered happily to Glory, telling her about friends at school and things she was going to do with her father. Only once did her small face cloud over.

"I like having dinner with you," she confided. "You talk to me. Mrs. Maxwell just sits at the table and reads the paper. Could I come over here when my daddy isn't home?"

Glory's heart went out to the lonely little girl. Bryan was doing the best he could, but the poor child needed a mother. She forced a smile. "I'm not home all the time myself, but we'll certainly do this again."

After dinner they watched television for a while, then Steffie put on her nightgown and got into Glory's bed without argument. She was so anxious to please that it was pathetic.

Glory brooded about it as she tried to get interested in a silly comedy show. The solution of course was for Bryan to marry again, but at this point, it didn't seem likely.

The telephone interrupted her fruitless speculation. Glory's eyes brightened as she went to answer it, certain that it was Darcy. He wasn't usually able to call until later, so this was an unexpected treat. It turned out not to be. Glory's mother greeted her, so upset she was almost incoherent.

"Calm down, Mother. I can't understand you. What's wrong with Dad?"

"I think he's having a heart attack. He's all doubled over and I don't know what to do!"

"You have to get him to the hospital immediately."

"He won't go—you know how stubborn your father is! Oh, Glory, can you come over right away?"

"Of course I will. But first call the paramedics. Dial them this minute, and I'll be there as soon as I can. Everything's going to be all right. Just don't panic."

After she hung up, Glory realized she had no way of getting there; a taxi would take ages to show up. Then there was Steffie. She couldn't leave her alone. If only Ellen hadn't gone out!

Luckily she was still home. After Glory had explained, Ellen said soothingly, "Take my car and I'll baby-sit. Stay as long as you're needed. I'll hold down the fort here."

"You're a lifesaver!" Glory exclaimed. "Steffie shouldn't wake up, but if she does, just tell her who you are. And explain to Bryan. He should be here any minute."

"Go!" Ellen pushed her out the door. "Everything will be fine here. I get along with kids, and I'll even try to be civil to her father, for your sake."

CHAPTER EIGHT

Bryan arrived shortly after Glory left. He was concerned over her father and apologetic about inconveniencing Ellen.

"It's all right," she said grudgingly. "I didn't have anything else to do."

"I know that isn't so, but it's good of you to say it. Glory said you were a nice person."

Ellen shot him a suspicious look, but Bryan's pleasant face was guileless. "What else did she tell you about me?"

"Not much, actually. Just that you were a lot of fun and she felt fortunate to have you as a neighbor."

"Glory sees a little good in everybody," Ellen muttered.

"She's something else, isn't she?" Bryan's smile changed to a worried frown. "I hope it's nothing serious with her father. If you don't mind, I'd like to wait and find out."

"Do you know him?"

"No, but Glory might need some help. You can go home if you like. I'll take over."

"I couldn't sleep until I heard either. Why don't I make some coffee? It might be a long night."

Bryan sat at the kitchen table, watching Ellen fill the percolator and put cookies on a plate. "This is nice. It reminds me of the times my wife used to fix us a snack before going to bed." He looked pensive. "That's one of the things I miss most about being married—the companionable times together."

"A man can usually get all the companionship he wants," Ellen replied curtly, pouring cream in a pitcher.

He shook his head. "We're talking about different things. Even if I had time to chase around, it isn't what I want. Once you've been happily married you know how important it is to care for someone and have her care for you. Casual encounters are no substitute for that."

"I'm glad you said *happily* married," Ellen commented dryly.

After a searching look at her sardonic face, Bryan murmured, "I'm sorry it didn't work out for you. I didn't mean to open up old wounds."

Ellen was unexpectedly touched. Here was a man who had lost a wife he obviously adored, and he was worried about hurting someone else's feelings! Although she told herself it wasn't such a big deal, her voice was softer as she said, "It's ancient history now. I never think about him."

"I think about Joanie all the time," Bryan answered quietly. "Memories can be very comforting."

"They can also be a trap. I doubt that your wife would want you to stop living."

"I'm not," he protested. "I have Steffie . . . and my work."

Ellen poured two cups of coffee. After carrying them to the table, she sat down across from Bryan. "If that's enough for you, you're different from any man *I* ever met."

"There isn't much I can do about it," he replied simply. "Not very many women are willing to wait until a little girl's needs are satisfied first."

"That's nonsense! Anyone that selfish isn't worth bothering about. There are a whole lot of others who would be more understanding."

"Would you?"

Ellen looked startled. "Would I what?"

"Would you go out with me some evening even though it might be rather late?"

"Well . . . I . . ."

Bryan's smile was a trifle lopsided. "You see?"

"It isn't that at all!" Ellen's normal composure deserted her. "I wouldn't mind how late it was . . . or where we went. It's just that I . . . Well, I don't go out much."

"It's okay, Ellen."

He reached out to pat her hand, and she realized with a sense of shock that this was the first time she hadn't felt like flinching away from a male touch. He was so damn . . . *nice!*

Bryan's smile was endearing. "I didn't mean to put you on the spot."

"You didn't, really!" It became important to her to convince him that her rejection was nothing personal. "I'm afraid I wasn't completely honest with you, Bryan. My marriage left some deep scars. I've avoided men as much as possible since the divorce. So you see, it has nothing to do with you."

"It must have been a pretty bad experience."

"It was," she said grimly. "He left me emotionally bankrupt."

"I don't believe that. You couldn't be as good a friend to Glory as you've been if you weren't capable of feeling."

"I didn't say I couldn't be a friend."

His eyes crinkled at the corners. "That's all I'm asking. I'm too out of practice for a fast start."

She returned his smile unwillingly. "It would come back to you. That's something you never forget—like riding a bicycle."

"If I promise to act like a big brother, will you go to Disneyland with Steffie and me on Saturday?"

"Are you sure that's what you want?" she asked doubtfully. "I'm not very relaxed around men, and I have a sharp tongue when I feel threatened."

"The only thing that could threaten you on Saturday is Mickey Mouse, and I'll keep the little varmint away from you."

The emotions racing through Ellen were ones she hadn't felt in a long time. She tried to tell herself that she had missed male company more than she realized, but deep down, Ellen knew that wasn't the reason for her increased pulse rate. Bryan's boyish good looks and caring manner had appealed to her immediately. Besides being attractive, he had all the attributes she liked in a man—good manners, intelligence, a sense of humor. Nothing would come of it, certainly, but there was no harm in going out with him.

Ellen didn't know that her eyes had taken on a becoming sparkle as she and Bryan sat over their coffee. They were deep in conversation when Glory returned.

Ellen sprang up to greet her, feeling guilty. She hadn't given her friend a thought for hours. "How is your father?"

"He'll be all right, thank goodness! It was food poisoning from something he ate at work, but Mother went all to pieces. I had to wait at the hospital until she calmed down a little. I'm sorry to have kept you both so late." She handed the car keys to Ellen.

"We're just glad it wasn't serious," Ellen said.

Glory turned to Bryan. "It was sweet of you to be concerned, but you didn't have to stay."

"I didn't mind. It gave me a chance to get acquainted with Ellen. I'll take Steffie home now."

When he left the room Glory said, "Thanks for keeping your promise about being civil to Bryan."

"As you can see, he doesn't have a claw mark on him." Ellen's laugh was strangely bubbly. She seemed to realize it because she hastily added, "Well, I'll be going now, too."

Glory stared after her with a thoughtful expression until Bryan's appearance with the sleeping child in his arms drove speculation from her mind. After they left, Glory was too drained emotionally to think about either of them that evening.

It seemed to Glory that Ellen was avoiding her the next couple of days. She was friendly enough, yet she always seemed to be in too big a hurry to stop and talk. Glory was faintly puzzled, but she was too excited about the upcoming weekend to give it much thought.

By the time Saturday finally arrived she was a bundle of nerves, certain that something would come up to prevent their trip. It wasn't until they checked into the hotel in Reno that she really believed it would happen.

Bryan had been forced to make reservations for them in Reno because the lodge at Lake Tahoe was full. It was about an hour's drive away, but in some ways, that was better. Darcy wouldn't be as easily accessible to all the people who wanted to lionize him.

When Darcy found out that he had a suite while Glory had only a room next door, he wanted to change with her, but she refused, pointing out the difficulties. He got phone calls at all hours. If she answered the phone late at night, how would it look?

"I'll just have them switch the calls," he answered.

"No, don't make waves. They'll get them mixed up and it could cause talk."

"How many times do I have to tell you that I don't give a damn?"

They were in Glory's room. They had just checked in and her suitcase was sitting unopened on the luggage rack where the bellman had left it.

Darcy took her in his arms with a sigh of contentment. "Do you know how long I've waited for this moment?" His lips were barely grazing hers. "Did you look forward to it, too, sweetheart?"

"More than you know," she whispered.

His arms tightened and his mouth closed over hers with a hunger born of denial. Darcy's tongue explored the moist recesses of her mouth, tracing the inside of her lower lip in a slow, sensuous path of discovery.

When she put her arms around his neck and ran her fingers through his thick dark hair, his tongue plunged deeper. He played on her senses, arousing her with promises of untold delights.

But when his hand lovingly cupped her breast, Glory tried to draw away. He pulled her back gently, burying his face in the brightness of her hair.

As his fingers found her sensitive nipple and stroked it lingeringly Darcy said in a husky voice, "Please let me touch you, darling. I've dreamed of nothing else for days."

Glory didn't know where she found the strength, but she removed his caressing hand. "It's one o'clock," she said breathlessly.

"A fantastic number." His mouth slid down her cheek, pausing at her ear. He blew into it softly. "You're number one, little angel."

"Darcy, please!" She held him off with difficulty. "We're due at that party at two thirty. It's an hour's drive, and we haven't unpacked yet."

His tongue traced the delicate inner curves of her ear. "Forget the party, forget the unpacking. I want to touch you and taste you. I could get drunk on the perfume of your skin."

"You promised," she insisted weakly. "People are working very hard on your campaign. You can't let them down."

Her words finally penetrated. He raised his head slowly, staring at her with a sense of incredulity. "What's happening to me, Glory? I've been a responsible person all my life. I pride myself on being dependable and loyal—all the Boy Scout virtues. But when I'm near you, nothing else seems to matter."

The self-condemnation in his voice chilled her. Was Darcy regretting their involvement? There was no doubt that it was undermining his performance. At a time when all his energies should be going into the campaign, his loyalties were divided. It had suddenly occurred to Darcy that he was acting completely out of character because of her.

"I should have stayed out of your life," she said miserably.

"Don't say that!" He crushed her in his arms. Tangling his fingers in her hair, he tugged her head back so he could look into her face. "You're the most wonderful thing that has ever happened to me."

"No." Tears glistened in Glory's eyes. "I'm jeopardizing your whole future."

Darcy's intense expression was replaced by a secret smile. His clutching fingers loosened and he smoothed her ruffled hair tenderly. "I think I have a solution for that, because we obviously have to do *something.* When we get back tonight, you and I are going to have a serious talk."

As he walked to the door Glory called, "Darcy, wait! What—"

"Weren't you the one who said we mustn't be late? I'll give you ten minutes to change clothes."

She stared after him, her thoughts in a turmoil. What did Darcy have to say to her? He had practically admitted she was a threat to his career. Was he going to suggest that it would be better if she left the campaign? His hunger for her made that seem impossible, but maybe he meant to satisfy it once and for all this weekend. It might be enough for him, but it wasn't for her. Glory's heart plunged as she faced a future without Darcy.

He avoided talking about anything personal on the

drive to the lake, so Glory did, too. There was no point in starting something they wouldn't have time to finish. Besides, Darcy didn't need an emotional scene right before he was due to be put on the grill. Not that Glory intended to make a scene. She loved him enough to put his welfare before her happiness.

"You're very quiet." He glanced over at her.

"I was just enjoying the beautiful scenery." They were driving on a winding mountain road that cut through dense stands of dark green pines and fir trees. "It must be gorgeous in winter with all the snow on the mountains. It's funny, but people never connect California with snow."

"That's what provides the water." Darcy looked thoughtful. "I'm going to face some tough questions on the south's proposal to divert northern streams."

Campaign issues took care of the conversation until they turned down Lake Shore Drive to one of the big estates that faced the sparkling water.

The party was in progress on the rolling green lawn in front of a large redwood and fieldstone house. People were dressed casually, but the women wore impressive jewels with their summer cottons. The talk was mostly about social events, past and future.

Glory began to doubt the importance of Darcy's being there until she met the inner circle. These were the leaders Bryan had spoken of. They asked intelligent probing questions and listened carefully to the answers. If Darcy managed to convince them, they could swing impressive weight behind him.

When the time came for the candidates to speak, folding chairs were set up on the lawn. After the first few speakers, Glory began to relax. Darcy shone by comparison like a diamond in a dirt heap, as she had known he would.

Glory's heart swelled with pride as she watched people surround him after his speech. He was so handsome, so charming. Yet Darcy never gave easy answers, the ones people wanted to hear. He was quietly adamant about basic rights. For the first time, Glory realized that it would be a great deal more than a personal triumph if Darcy were elected. He could do a great deal of good.

She was euphoric in the car going back to Reno after they finally managed to pry themselves away from the party. "You won that one hands down," she crowed. "The others looked like baggy pants comics next to you."

Darcy chuckled. "You wouldn't be a little bit prejudiced, would you?"

"I'm a whole *lot* prejudiced, but that doesn't change the facts. Those people loved you!"

"I hope they remember that when November rolls around."

"Don't be such a cynic! Why won't you admit that the election is practically in the bag?"

"Because it isn't, honey." Darcy was suddenly serious. "Any amount of unforeseen things could happen. The public is remarkably judgmental about politicians. We aren't allowed the benefit of the doubt like other people."

"Nothing's going to happen," she assured him. "For one thing, you *look* more like a state senator than any of the others."

Darcy's white teeth showed in a broad grin. "Why didn't you say that in the first place? Now *there's* a bit of scientific reasoning I can relate to."

When they returned to the hotel and went to the front desk for their keys, sounds from the casino filled the lobby. Croupiers called out numbers at the roulette wheels and dice tables, and the enticing clatter of coins jingling into metal cups announced fortunate winners at the slot machines.

Glory turned an animated face to Darcy. "Can we play for a little while? I feel lucky."

"Casino owners get rich on statements like that," he remarked dryly, but he put his arm around her and led her into the busy room.

When she decided to try the slot machines, Darcy bought her enough coins to fill a paper cup. Then he wandered off to try his hand at the dice table.

In spite of her expressed feeling, Glory wasn't especially lucky. She won a few coins at a time but put more back. Her cup was almost empty when suddenly bells sounded and flashing lights lighted the slot machine. She was looking slightly dazed when a man in a black apron came over to tell her she'd won the Lucky Nugget jackpot.

"I won a thousand dollars!" she told Darcy a few moments later, throwing her arms around his neck. "I told you I felt lucky!"

"I'm sharing in it," he grinned as he held her slender body close.

"We have to celebrate," she declared.

"How about opening that bottle of champagne the management left in the suite?" he suggested.

Darcy's suite wasn't as plush as those in big city hotels, but it was furnished comfortably with a couch and several chairs in the living room. After he had poured the champagne, he raised his glass to Glory. "What are you going to do with your windfall?"

She looked at him blankly. "I was so excited about winning that spending it never occurred to me."

Darcy smiled fondly. "You certainly aren't typical. Most women would already have it earmarked for jewelry—or perhaps a trip to glamorous places."

"I've never cared for jewelry." Marshall had always insisted that she wear obviously expensive pieces that would advertise his wealth. She had left it all behind her.

"Don't you like to travel, either?"

She shrugged. "I haven't really thought about it."

"There must be *some* place you'd like to go," he persisted.

Was she imagining it or was there a purpose behind Darcy's questions? Was he using this as an opportunity to ease her out without embarrassing apologies? Glory had to admit it made sense.

She gripped her champagne glass tightly. "A trip does sound nice—perhaps one of those luxury cruises."

"Where would you like to go?"

"Oh . . . Hawaii maybe. I've never been there."

"It's beautiful. Palm trees waving over blue water, pretty hula girls in grass skirts."

"They'd appeal to you more than to me." Glory was staring down into her glass, so she didn't see the expression on Darcy's face.

"Not if you were anywhere around," he said huskily.

She wasn't in the mood for empty compliments. "Do you think I'll have trouble getting reservations?"

"I'll take care of it."

"I could leave as soon as possible," she said tonelessly.

Darcy frowned. "You know that isn't practical, honey."

No, she couldn't leave him in the lurch. Someone would have to be trained to take her place. Glory only hoped she could make it through the transition period.

She sighed deeply. "Well, at the earliest opportunity, then."

"There's no way I can get away until after the election."

She looked up, startled out of her misery. "What does that have to do with it?"

"Were you planning to go on our honeymoon without me?"

"I—I don't understand."

Darcy put his glass on the coffee table and moved over to take her in his arms. "I suppose it's polite to ask first. You *will* marry me, won't you, angel?" He kissed the tip of her nose. "I warn you that a wrong answer is subject to appeal."

"But I thought . . . You said . . ."

Darcy seemed more interested in the tiny kisses he was feathering all over her face. "What did I say, sweetheart?"

"You said I was disrupting your career!"

"No, *you* said that—although I have to agree with you. I've never been this way before. My work, the campaign—everything is unimportant next to you!" He strained to pull her close. "I *need* you, Glory. Without you none of this means anything. Please say you'll marry me, darling."

Her eyes were dazed as she pulled back enough to look up at him. "I thought you were sending me away."

"You didn't! How could you think such a thing? Haven't I been acting like a lovesick schoolboy, phoning at midnight, blowing my stack when our dates were canceled? I'm a classic example of a frustrated male yearning for his mate."

"But I thought you only—" She stopped abruptly. What difference did it make now? Glory's heart was pounding with the realization that Darcy loved her! The swing from misery to ecstasy was dizzying.

"You thought I only wanted to take you to bed?" Darcy asked, almost sternly. "Didn't you ever listen when I told you I wanted to share *everything* with you? Yes, I want your beautiful body, but I want so much more."

Tears made Glory's eyes emerald bright. "Oh, Darcy, I love you so!"

His mouth crushed hers in wild triumph. "I don't know what I would have done if you'd said no," he groaned when he finally released her. "I couldn't stay away from you if I tried." His hands wandered restlessly over her back, molding the gentle curves of her waist and hips. "Promise you'll never leave me, my love."

Framing his beloved face between her palms, Glory stared into his ardent eyes. "How could I?" she whispered.

"You're mine!" he said passionately. "Every exquisite inch of you."

With a sudden movement, he swung her into his arms and stood up. Their eyes held as he carried her into the bedroom. When he lowered her to her feet beside the king-size bed, Glory's legs were trembling.

Darcy's kiss was unexpectedly chaste. "Don't be frightened, angel. I'll be gentle with you."

"I know that, and I'm not afraid." She unbuttoned his shirt and raked her nails lightly through the curling black hair on his broad chest. "I'm a woman, Darcy. I want you to make love to me without holding anything back. I've never really been loved before."

Darcy's kiss was deep and satisfying. His tongue was demanding and exciting. He slid her zipper down without releasing her mouth. Her dress slid to the floor, followed by her bra.

Darcy's hands smoothed the silken skin of her back, then cupped her breasts. Glory drew in her breath sharply as his thumbs made slow circles over her nipples. When they curled into little rosettes, he bent his head and took one in his mouth. Golden sparks ignited inside Glory as his wet tongue and warm lips caressed each sensitive peak. She clutched at his broad shoulders, moaning softly.

Darcy lifted his head to gaze at her with blazing eyes. "I knew it would be like this!" He held her at arm's length. "Let me look at you—all of you."

Glory wore only a pair of lace bikini panties and high-heeled sandals. Under Darcy's ardent gaze she felt her body heating to a boiling point. When he knelt to unbuckle her shoes, she tangled her fingers in his dark hair to keep her balance.

After she stepped out of them, Darcy remained kneeling in front of her. His palms slid slowly up her legs, tracing the shapely curves. When his fingertips slipped inside the elastic of her bikini, the sparks became embers that threatened to burst into flames.

"Darcy, please! Do you know what you're doing to me?" she gasped.

He chuckled softly. "I hope so."

He removed her panties and lifted her onto the bed. Glory pulled him down beside her and molded her body to his lean length. Her mouth searched for his as she moved against him, crushing her breasts against the hard wall of his chest.

Darcy's legs scissored around hers, pinning her tightly. His hand cupped her bottom, urging her against the taut vee of his thighs. Glory had never known such hunger. She slipped her hands inside the waistband of his slacks and dug her nails into his buttocks.

"I didn't know it could be like this," she murmured.

"My lovely, passionate Glory!"

Darcy's mouth held hers as he struggled out of his shirt. He left her for just a moment to fling off the rest of his clothes, then returned and took her in his arms once more. The feeling of his splendid, naked male body against her own bare skin was incendiary. Glory ran her hands over him, wanting to experience every part of him.

A shudder went through Darcy at her feathery touch. Uttering a wordless cry, he moved over her and parted her legs. Clasping her in his arms, he completed their union. The exquisite sensation filled Glory with such pleasure that she arched her body into his.

He was the center of her world, the purveyor of rapture she had never known. She clung to him as her passion soared, carrying her to dizzying heights. Every thrust of his body brought almost unbelievable excitement. The exquisite climax was a storm of emotion that spread throughout her entire being.

Darcy held her close as the waves of feeling swept through them. The storm gradually diminished in receding waves that left Glory completely and utterly fulfilled. She was cradled in his arms, safe and protected—and loved.

Neither moved for a long time. When she finally stirred, Darcy's arms tightened. "If you think you're getting away from me, you're mistaken," he growled. "I might keep you in this bed all weekend."

She laughed softly. "That's what I had planned all along."

"You brought me up here to seduce me?"

"It seemed the only way," she said mischievously. "I wasn't making any headway in the city."

"That's all going to change." Darcy's voice was very firm. "From now on you're going to be with me day *and* night." He scowled. "I wish you could move into my apartment, but I don't suppose it would be a good idea."

"Certainly not!" she gasped. "Are you *trying* to lose the election?"

"I wasn't thinking about that," he answered negligently. "I just don't want to jeopardize your divorce."

"You won't. Because I refuse to live with you until you make an honest woman of me," she teased.

"Can we visit a lot?" He stroked her thigh suggestively.

"What do you think?"

Any problems the future might hold seemed very unimportant when Darcy's hands and body began to work their wondrous magic.

CHAPTER NINE

It was the most idyllic weekend of Glory's life. She and Darcy swam in the hotel pool and had dinner by candlelight in his suite. They talked and laughed together, and they made love—passionate, fulfilling love. Glory reached undreamed of heights as Darcy initiated her into a world of unparalleled sensation.

He was a tender yet masterful lover. His greatest delight was pleasing her, and he searched out every possible way. They fell asleep in each other's arms and awoke in the same position, as though they couldn't bear to be parted. It was an enchanted time.

They stretched it out as long as possible by taking the evening plane back to Los Angeles.

"I wish you'd let me announce our engagement," Darcy complained as he was driving her home from the airport. His handsome face wore a look of dissatisfaction.

"We've been over all that," Glory said patiently. "We decided it wouldn't be a good idea."

"No. *You* decided. I want everyone to know you belong to me, but you won't even let me buy you a ring."

She covered his hand with hers. "*We* know how much we love each other—that's all that matters." Her smile held a tinge of sadness. "If my notorious past hurt you at the polls, Bryan would never forgive us."

"Why do I have to keep telling you that you're the most important thing in my life?" Darcy demanded as he braked in front of her apartment.

"Because I like hearing it." Glory lifted her face for his kiss. "Go home and get a good night's sleep. That's the only thing that was in short supply this weekend."

"The weekend isn't over yet," he murmured huskily. "How about staying at my place tonight?"

It was a temptation when his tongue slipped suggestively between her lips and his hand caressed her body. But Glory knew that Darcy had work to prepare for the next day. He couldn't go without sleep indefinitely. She reminded him of it and stood firm against all his arguments. If he didn't have sense enough to do what was best for him, she'd have to do it for him.

Ellen offered Glory a ride to work the next morning when they happened to meet in the hallway.

"How was your weekend with the wealthy?" Ellen asked as they drove down Olympic Boulevard. The glow on Glory's face would have given her the answer, but Ellen was intent on the early morning traffic.

"Very luxurious." Glory answered her friend's question lightly. "Those people subscribe to Samuel Johnson's theory that it's better to live rich than die rich. You never saw so much jewelry in your life."

Glory really wanted to tell Ellen about her engagement, but two things prevented her. True, it was important to keep it a secret for Darcy's sake. But perhaps the main reason was that she didn't want to hear another of Ellen's tirades against men. Not after the tenderness Darcy displayed. She couldn't resist talking about him, though. Glory's voice was soft as she related his triumph at the garden party.

"Bryan said he's a rare bird," Ellen observed grudgingly.

Glory raised her eyebrows. "You're willing to take his word for it and not mine? That's a switch."

"Well, he—uh—seems like such a decent person, Bryan, I mean."

"You discovered that in just the short time you two were together the other night?"

"No, he . . . um . . . stopped by last Saturday with his little girl." Before Glory could make more than a surprised exclamation, they pulled up in front of campaign headquarters. Ellen said hurriedly, "I'm really in a rush. See you later."

Glory stared after the departing car. Ellen and Bryan? Her mouth curved in a smile as she went inside.

The following weeks were as busy as they were happy. True to his word, Darcy insisted that Glory accompany him everywhere. She was a little worried about being so visible, but she hoped her position in the campaign would provide an excuse.

On Darcy's rare free nights they usually had dinner at his apartment, sometimes after a couple of sets of tennis to help him unwind.

They were having coffee in the living room on one of those nights, talking about Bryan's surprising romance with Ellen. Curling more comfortably in Darcy's arms, Glory remarked, "Ellen's a completely different person."

Darcy kissed her temple. "Shall I say the obvious? That any change would be an improvement?"

Glory sighed. "If you two ever got to know each other, you'd change your opinions."

"We already agree on all the important things." Darcy grinned. "She detests me, and I can't stand her."

"If something comes of her relationship with Bryan, you'll have to learn to get along with her."

"I expect Bryan to come to his senses. Love might be blind, but it isn't feebleminded."

Glory didn't bother to argue with him. She was working on a plan. "You haven't been down to the Malibu house in ages," she remarked in an abrupt change of subject. "Why don't we have a picnic on the beach next Sunday?"

"A noble idea." Darcy lifted the long hair away from her ear and started to explore the inner cavity with his tongue.

She refused to be distracted, although his mouth was tantalizing. "We could invite Bryan and Ellen to join us."

"No!" Darcy's answer was immediate and unequivocal. "I'm not wasting what little time we have together with that card-carrying man-hater."

"Please, Darcy, for my sake? She's my friend."

He groaned as he gazed down into her lovely pleading face. Swinging her onto his lap, he said, "You know I can't deny you anything."

Glory put her arms around his neck and kissed the hollow at the base of his throat. "One favor deserves another. Is there anything I can do to please *you?*"

"I can't think of anything that doesn't!" His hands slipped under the hem of her T-shirt to cup the fullness of both bare breasts. "I'm especially enamored of your anatomy."

She tugged his T-shirt out of his shorts and pushed it up under his arms. "Yours is pretty spectacular, too," she commented, running her fingertips over his lean chest.

Darcy pulled the shirt over his head, then removed Glory's. They were both left with only matching white tennis shorts. He bent his head and kissed her stiffening nipples, then rolled them between his lips. Glory stroked his dark hair as tiny flames kindled within her.

"I want to please you in every way a man can please a woman," he murmured, feathering her breasts with intoxicating kisses.

"You do, darling," Glory said faintly. She closed her eyes to savor the intense feeling.

He placed her full length on the couch and knelt with

one knee on either side of her. After staring at the perfection of her body, Darcy stroked her silken skin from her collarbone to her waist. His mouth followed the same path, trailing kisses that turned Glory liquid inside. When he tugged gently at her waistband to expose her navel, then dipped his tongue in the little depression, she murmured his name softly.

"Yes, my love, tell me what you want," he said hoarsely.

He slid her shorts down slowly, kissing the golden skin, then the strip of pale skin that was usually hidden. After her shorts were removed completely, Darcy gently lifted her leg. His warm mouth burned a path over the soft skin of her inner thigh.

Glory arched her body. "Oh, Darcy, I want *you!*" she gasped.

"You'll always have me, sweetheart."

His shorts followed hers to the floor in a blur of motion. Darcy's urgency matched Glory's as he lowered his hard body to hers. She met his driving masculine force with a passion that mounted with every tempestuous movement. When her tension reached the breaking point, it burst in a flash of splendor that could only be experienced, not described.

Afterward they lay in each other's arms, completely, happily spent. Darcy finally broke the contented silence. "You're sure you want to invite other people next Sunday?"

"It's only for the afternoon," she consoled him, kissing the point of his chin. "They'll have Steffie with them, so they'll have to leave early."

"And if they don't?"

"It will work out. You'll see," she said confidently. "Every problem has a solution."

"Sure, but some are damned hard to live with," he grumbled.

Much later, Glory was to remember those words.

* * *

In spite of her assurances to Darcy that he and Ellen would grow to like each other, Glory was nervous about the picnic. They were both such strong people.

Ellen had only consented to come because she wanted to be with Bryan. She seemed genuinely in love with him, although she stopped short of admitting it. Ellen was less abrasive, however. If only she and Darcy didn't strike sparks off each other.

Glory and Darcy were getting things ready in the kitchen of the beach house when Steffie's excited voice announced her arrival. She burst in with hugs and kisses while Bryan and Ellen were getting their things from the car.

Steffie's presence helped to ease whatever awkwardness might have developed. She adored Darcy and monopolized him for the first few minutes.

After telling him about nursery school and their new kitten, she held up a tiny bathing suit. "Aunt Ellen bought me this just for today."

Ellen flushed slightly. "It was a sample one of the salesmen left," she mumbled.

"I have to show Aunt Ellen the ocean," Steffie announced importantly, taking her hand. "She hasn't been here before and I have."

When they'd gone down the steps to the beach, Bryan said fondly, "Steffie's been in seventh heaven lately. She's wild about Ellen."

"Who says you can't buy love?" Darcy remarked cynically.

"You should be ashamed of yourself!" Glory scolded. "Ellen, of *all* people, doesn't have an ulterior motive."

"She's right," Bryan agreed. "I know you and Ellen didn't hit it off, but she's a wonderful person when you get to know her."

Although he didn't appear convinced, Darcy stifled the reply he wanted to make.

154

It was late in the afternoon when Darcy and Ellen found themselves alone on the beach blanket. The other two were paddling in the surf with Steffie.

"Are you serious about Glory?" Ellen asked abruptly.

"The answer to that question should be obvious."

She glanced toward the water at Glory's faultless figure in a tiny yellow bikini. "She's gorgeous," Ellen said. She turned her head to look squarely at Darcy. "But that's not what I'm talking about."

He raised a dark eyebrow. "Are you asking me if my intentions are honorable?"

She hesitated a moment. "I know it's none of my business, but I'm so fond of her. I don't want to see her get hurt."

Darcy's eyes moved irresistibly to Glory. His face filled with a kind of wonder as he gazed at her bright hair and delicate profile.

"I love her," he said quietly. "Glory doesn't want anyone to know yet, but we're going to be married as soon as her divorce is final."

Ellen's tense body relaxed. "Oh, Darcy, I'm so happy for you both!" She grinned suddenly. "Did you ever think you'd hear that from *me?*"

He returned her smile. "No, but I never thought we'd be sitting here without our fencing masks either. I guess two people who both love Glory can't be all bad."

After the weekend, Glory convinced Darcy that they needed an early evening. The week ahead was going to be a busy one.

That Monday night she fixed herself a light dinner, then showered and got into her nightgown and robe. She was curled up in a chair reading when Ellen tapped on the door.

"Oh, are you going to bed so early?" Ellen eyed

Glory's nightclothes. "I saw your lights on and thought I'd come in and visit for a while."

"I was just reading," Glory assured her. "Come on in."

They talked about the picnic the day before and the fact that summer was almost over. But throughout the casual conversation, Glory got the impression that Ellen was distracted. There was an air of suppressed emotion, a feeling of tension about her. Finally she voiced what was on her mind.

"Bryan asked me to marry him," she blurted out suddenly.

"That's wonderful!" Glory exclaimed. "You accepted, I hope."

Ellen's smile was blissful. "I barely let him finish his proposal."

"Well, I'm glad to see you finally showed some common sense. Bryan is a living doll."

"He's given me back my faith in the male sex," Ellen said softly. "I didn't think he could possibly be interested in me. It was too much to hope for. The first couple of weeks I told myself he was only looking for a sleep-in mother for Steffie." A shadow of doubt clouded her face. "You don't suppose I'm just kidding myself?"

"You know better than that. Bryan is crazy about you! His feelings couldn't have been more obvious yesterday."

"It's just that I made such a terrible mistake the first time," Ellen said soberly.

"So did I, but at least it taught me to recognize real love when I was lucky enough to find it."

"Darcy told me you were engaged. I hope you don't mind. He said you wanted to keep it a secret."

"Not from you." Glory grinned. "I would have told you myself, but I didn't want to sit through another lecture on the duplicity of men and their lying, cheating ways."

156

Ellen smiled ruefully. "I was something of a pain in the posterior, wasn't I?"

"Well, let's just say it was like trying to win an argument with the I.R.S."

Ellen shook her head, remembering. "I was that way with Bryan, too, in the beginning. I wonder why he bothered with me?"

"The fact that he was willing to risk a severe case of frostbite proves it's love," Glory teased. "When are you getting married?"

"Not until after the election. Bryan is so tied up with the campaign that it's only sensible to wait. How about you and Darcy?"

"We don't have any choice. My divorce isn't final yet. But even if it were, I wouldn't marry Darcy now." Glory looked troubled. "I'm not exactly an asset to him."

"Don't say that! Any man would be lucky to get you."

"Oh, sure. The notorious Glory Prescott—the girl who married for money, then ran out on her husband after three months."

"You know that's not the real story."

"But nobody else does." Glory's eyes were shadowed. "I worry about how it will affect Darcy after he's elected."

"They'd scarcely get out a recall petition because he married you," Ellen observed dryly.

"No, but the state senate is only the beginning. Darcy has a brilliant future ahead of him. If I thought I was a danger to it, I'd walk out of his life for good."

"You'll be the best thing that ever happened to his career. Besides, he'd never let you go."

"That's what worries me. Darcy wouldn't think twice about sacrificing himself for me if it came to a choice."

"It isn't going to, so stop borrowing trouble. Just relax and count your blessings."

"I suppose you're right." Glory shivered suddenly. "Everything is so perfect that I guess I'm afraid it can't last."

"It probably won't for more than thirty or forty years," Ellen returned, smiling.

The weeks that followed were so unbelievably happy that Glory forgot her apprehensions. The opinion polls showed Darcy far in the lead, and their wedding date grew closer with every passing day. There wasn't a cloud in the sky.

Then, just when life seemed perfect, an item appeared in a local gossip column. It read:

That handsome bachelor candidate Darcy Lord isn't giving all his attention to the race for state senate. Some of it is going to his gorgeous assistant, Glory Prescott. He can't keep his . . . eyes . . . off her. In case the name sounds familiar, she's the same Glory Prescott who was wed to Marshall Wentworth not long ago in the social event of the season. Let's hope this romance lasts longer than that marriage.

Glory found out about the item when a reporter called her for a comment. She hadn't had time to read the paper that morning and wouldn't have bothered with that column anyway. It was written by a man who specialized in titillating bits of innuendo that always managed to stop just short of being libelous. Naturally the column was very popular.

After getting rid of the persistent reporter, Glory grabbed the morning paper. She was reading the article with a stricken expression when Darcy stopped at her desk.

He curled his hand around the nape of her neck. "You look so serious. What's the matter? Did Garfield

158

the cat go off his diet?" When she raised her face to his, Darcy's smile faded. "What is it, honey?"

She handed him the newspaper without trusting herself to answer.

Darcy looked disgusted as he finished the short squib. He threw the paper in the wastebasket. "This is where garbage like that belongs!"

Glory's eyes were dark pools of misery. "I was so afraid this would happen. I never should have let myself be seen with you so often."

"That's nonsense! I'm glad it's out in the open. Now maybe you'll let me announce our engagement."

"Darcy, no! That would make it even worse! At least that item makes it sound as though we're just . . . well, having a little fling."

"And you think I'll put up with it?" His mouth set in a grim line.

Darcy's fingers clamped around Glory's wrist. After pulling her to her feet, he led her into the small storeroom at the back of the office and closed the door.

His strong hands held her shoulders firmly. "Listen to me, Glory. I love you. I'm not ashamed of it. I don't care if the whole world finds out."

"We've talked about it," she said helplessly. "I could hurt you."

"Only if you stopped loving me." He shook her slightly. "You're not a criminal, sweetheart! You made a mistake—so what? If a few narrow-minded people hold it against you, that's their problem."

"I don't want them to hold it against *you!*"

"They won't. You're worrying for nothing. Sure, it will be unpleasant if the papers rehash your marriage, but it will blow over. In a few days they'll be hassling some other poor victim and everyone will have forgotten all about you."

"I wish I could believe that," she whispered.

"Trust me."

Darcy took her in his arms and molded her quivering body to his. She clung to him as he gently kissed her eyelids, the tip of her nose, her trembling mouth.

"I couldn't bear it if anything happened to you because of me," she said softly. "I love you so much."

Darcy uttered a wordless exclamation. His mouth became suddenly demanding as the passion that was always present between them flared. His hands roamed restlessly over Glory's slim body, urging her against the hard angles of his chest and thighs while his tongue plundered her mouth. She surrendered completely, winding her arms around his neck.

After a long moment Darcy groaned and buried his face in the scented cloud of her hair. "In another minute I'm going to take you right here. Do you know how much I want you?"

Glory drew back to gaze up at him with a tender smile. "About half as much as I want you."

Darcy's hands tightened on her shoulders as he started to pull her back in his arms. He checked himself with an effort. "If you keep looking at me like that, I won't be responsible for my own actions, and then what will people think? It's a good thing we're announcing our engagement."

Her smile changed to concern. "You can't do that, Darcy!"

"Just watch me! If they want something to write about, I'll give them a *real* story."

"No, please don't," she begged desperately. "You said yourself it would all die down if we just ignored it. But if you give them fuel to keep the fire going, they won't ever let us alone."

Darcy's eyes were like ice. "Anyone who tries to harass you will answer to me."

Glory looked despairingly at his lithe body and square jaw. She knew that any reporter or photographer would get the worst of a tangle with Darcy, but that would make it even more disastrous. She tried to reason with him. When that failed, she pleaded. Glory was emotionally drained when she finally persuaded Darcy to continue on the way they had been.

"I've never been furtive in my life," he said disgustedly. "But if it means that much, I'll go along with you." He lifted her chin and smiled down at her ruefully. "Maybe I'll lead the Senate someday, but there's sure no doubt about who's going to rule the roost at home."

"It's the right decision, Darcy," she said quietly.

His smile faded. "Is it? I wonder."

When several days passed and there was no further mention of her in the papers, Glory started to relax. She was alone in her apartment when the phone call came that was to shatter her life.

Marshall started quite pleasantly. "It's good to hear your voice, Glory. How've you been?"

"Fine, thanks. And you?" It was ridiculous to be exchanging pleasantries, but she didn't know what else to say.

"How's a man supposed to feel after his wife walked out on him?" he asked with a touch of venom.

Glory pretended not to hear it. "How is your grandmother?"

"Not too happy. She's been asking about you."

"Be sure and give her my love," Glory said politely.

"You gave that to *me* once." His voice deepened significantly.

Her skin crawled at the memory. "What do you want, Marshall?" she asked bluntly.

He gave a small laugh. "That isn't very friendly."

"We aren't friends," she stated flatly.

"No, we're married." There was mockery in his tone.

"Not anymore!"

"Oh, yes, we are, Glory." His voice was deceptively soft.

She felt the familiar sense of helplessness that Marshall always induced. "My attorney contacted you! You know I've filed for divorce."

"Yes, you were in quite a temper when you ran out on me that night." His calm attitude made it sound as though they'd had a simple argument. "But there's no harm done if it helped you get it out of your system."

Glory couldn't believe what she was hearing. "We're all through, Marshall! Our marriage was a terrible mistake."

"You didn't think so when I gave you a four-carat diamond engagement ring." His ugly tone made him sound like the man she remembered so well.

"I gave it back to you," she reminded him quietly.

"Did your new boyfriend offer you a bigger one?" he taunted.

Glory gripped the phone tightly. "This isn't getting us anywhere. I'm sorry if your pride was hurt because I left you, but that's *all* that was damaged. You never loved me, Marshall. I realize that now."

"Because this Lord guy is better in the sack?" he asked derisively. "He wants the same thing from you that I do, baby. At least it's legal with me."

A ripple of disgust shuddered up Glory's spine. "Not anymore, it isn't."

"I have an attorney, too," Marshall replied smugly. "And he tells me that technically all you have to do is come home and we'll be considered man and wife again."

"There isn't anything in this world that could make me go back to you!"

"I suppose you think it's more glamorous to be a senator's wife," Marshall sneered. "What makes you think he's going to marry you? Get smart, kid. He's only interested in the free samples you've been handing out."

Glory was so furious that the words tumbled out of her. "That's exactly the sort of thinking I'd expect from your dirty little mind! For your information, Darcy and I are being married just as soon as my divorce is final."

"You're really sure of yourself, aren't you? What if it were a choice between you and the state senate seat?"

"What do you mean?"

"How many votes do you think it would cost your lover boy if people knew he was the reason our marriage broke up after only three months?"

"I didn't even know him then!" she cried.

"You sure got acquainted fast—like the night you left me. I hear you two spent the weekend in Malibu together."

"But we didn't do—How did you know?" she whispered.

"I figured that's what happened!" he exclaimed triumphantly.

Glory realized with a sinking heart that she had just put a weapon in Marshall's hand. One that he wouldn't hesitate to use.

"I've got your boyfriend's career by the short hairs," Marshall bragged. "If I talk to the newspapers, he couldn't even get elected dog catcher."

"You can't do that! Darcy can do so much good. He's a dedicated man."

"Yeah, I know the type," Marshall said bitterly. "Mr. Popular. Well, he might not be the people's choice for much longer."

"Please don't do this." Glory fought to stem the flow of tears.

"It's up to you, baby. Come home like a good little girl, and we'll pretend nothing ever happened." He gave a nasty laugh. "If you're especially nice to me, I might even vote for the jerk."

Glory knew that Marshall would carry out his threat. He would do anything to get her back—not because he loved her but because he couldn't stand the thought of losing. It would be even worse this time. Could she go through with it? Glory blinked back the tears and stiffened her spine. She could do anything to protect Darcy.

"Well, how about it?" Marshall asked.

"You really are a slime," she said contemptuously.

"I wouldn't advise you to toss names around. There are a few I could use on you and your boyfriend."

"Call me anything you like," she replied tightly. "Just leave Darcy out of this."

"You can't have your fun without paying for it," Marshall taunted. "You know what the price tag is."

It was far too high, but if she didn't pay it Darcy would have to.

Glory's voice held grim determination as she surrendered all her future happiness. "Okay, you win. I'll come back. But only if you promise to leave Darcy alone."

"That's up to you." His voice was more menacing somehow because of its softness. "It all depends on how happy you keep me."

CHAPTER TEN

The dark circles under Glory's eyes attested to the sleepless night she'd spent after Marshall's phone call. She tried to camouflage them with makeup, but Darcy wasn't fooled.

"Don't you feel well, honey?" He stood by her desk, looking at her with concern.

"I have a slight headache," she said dismissively.

Her reply didn't satisfy him. "If it doesn't get better, I want you to go home. There's such a thing as being too conscientious." He put his hand gently on her hair.

It was almost more than Glory could take. Could she get through a whole week of being near him, now that he was forever out of reach? When she agreed to go back to Marshall, Glory had insisted on a week to train someone to take her job. Marshall had argued, but it was the one thing she was adamant about. They had a luncheon date that day, at *his* insistence.

"Maybe you'd better not go to the rally at Civic Center tonight," Darcy said. "Those things are always hectic."

"I think you're right," she agreed, not looking at him.

He frowned thoughtfully. "Is anything wrong, Glory?"

She forced a bright smile. "What could be wrong?"

He hesitated. "I don't know. You seem so . . . preoccupied."

"I have work to do. Not all of us can goof off like the boss." She tried to make the words sound jocular.

"I know when I'm not wanted." He laughed. "But you'll be sorry someday that you tried to get rid of me."

Glory didn't trust herself to answer. She watched mutely as he went into his office.

Darcy came out a little later to inquire about her headache and suggest lunch, but she put him off with an excuse. She was getting ready to leave for the restaurant when Marshall came into the office.

He looked disdainfully around the cluttered room. "So this is where you've been hanging out. Not a very classy joint, is it?"

Glory froze in her chair. "What are you doing here?" She cast an apprehensive glance toward Darcy's office, but he was deep in paperwork.

"I wanted to meet your ex-boyfriend. After all, we have a lot in common." Marshall leered suggestively.

"Leave him alone!" she ordered.

An ugly expression crossed Marshall's face. "You're in no position to tell me what to do."

Glory pushed her chair back and stood up to confront him. It flashed through her mind that she didn't have to look up to Marshall as she did to Darcy—in more ways than one. "I've agreed to your blackmail, but you can't have it both ways. Either you stay away from Darcy, or our deal is off."

One look at her icy green eyes told Marshall he had pushed Glory to the limit. He searched for a way to back down gracefully. "That isn't a very romantic way to refer to our reunion," he reproached her playfully.

"Is that what you call revenge and punishment?" she asked contemptuously.

"Okay, if that's the way you want it. I was willing to be civilized about this, but I can play rough, too." His thin mouth twisted in a snarl. "Just so you know the score. Did you tell him yet?"

166

"That has nothing to do with you."

"I thought so! You think you can play both ends against the middle, but it won't work, baby. I'm telling him right now! In a way, I'm glad you gave me the pleasure," he gloated.

"If you say one word to Darcy, you'll never get your filthy hands on me!" she warned, her body tense.

They were confronting each other so furiously that neither noticed Darcy's approach. His deep voice made Glory pale.

"What's going on?" Darcy demanded.

"Oh! I thought you were—" She stopped to compose herself. "This is Marshall Wentworth, my—my husband." The words almost choked her. It was the hardest thing Glory had ever done.

Neither man offered to shake hands. "I see." Darcy's face was expressionless. "Would you like me to escort him out of here?"

"No!" she said hastily. "I mean, we were just leaving."

"We?" Darcy stared at her incredulously.

"Yes, I . . . that is, Marshall and I are having lunch together."

"We'd ask you to join us, but you know how it is." Marshall's eyes gleamed with malicious enjoyment. "Glory and I haven't seen each other in so long. We want to talk about old times."

Darcy clenched his hands unconsciously. "Like the last time you saw her?"

"She told you about that?" Marshall's mean eyes promised retribution as they slanted toward Glory. "She always was a little bubble head, babbling everything she knows."

"I won't be long," Glory broke in desperately. "Tell Gretchen to cover the phones for me." The expression on Darcy's face would stay with her for a long time.

Glory was so mired in misery that Marshall's triumphant gloating in the car barely penetrated. She still had to face Darcy when she got back. How could she spare him the pain she was going through?

"I guess your boyfriend got the idea without either of us having to tell him," Marshall crowed. "Did you see the look on his face when I waltzed off with you?"

"Yes, I saw it," she answered quietly.

"What's the matter, baby? Feeling sorry for him? Don't worry—it won't take him long to find someone else."

Glory knew that Marshall was wrong. Darcy loved her deeply. If the situation were reversed, he would make the same sacrifice she was making. That's what made it not only worthwhile but imperative. Darcy was too fine a person to be destroyed by someone like Marshall.

It was true that he would eventually find someone else. After all, life did go on. But he would suffer greatly until the wound healed. Only one thing hurt as much as losing him: Darcy would always think he had misjudged her. Glory's eyes were bleak as she stared down at her tightly intertwined fingers.

"To show you I'm not such a bad guy, I'll even introduce him to some foxy girls I know. Sort of get him back in circulation." Marshall glanced over at her bowed head. "I haven't exactly been sitting home every night since you left."

"I'm sure you haven't." There was no bitterness in her answer. Glory simply didn't care.

"There were plenty of women happy to console me," he went on smugly. When she didn't comment, he said, "Maybe we'll give a party so Mr. Wonderful can meet them. Would you like that?"

"If you're trying to hurt me, Marshall, it's a waste of time. Go back to pulling wings off butterflies—or whatever you do for recreation. You've already done as much as you can to me."

"Don't count on it, sweetheart!" His mask fell away, revealing a bitter, thwarted man. "You made a fool of me in front of the whole world. That's something I'm not going to forget. You have exactly one week. Next Thursday night I'm coming to your apartment to get you. Be ready!"

Darcy was waiting for her when she got back to the office, as Glory knew he would be. He didn't waste any time on amenities.

"Will you tell me what the hell is going on?" Darcy demanded.

Glory took as much time as possible putting her purse in the bottom drawer of her desk. It gave her an opportunity to avoid looking at him. "What do you mean?"

"What was that little creep doing here? And why wouldn't you let me throw him out?"

"We never rough up a potential voter," she said lightly.

Darcy grasped her shoulders, forcing her to face him. "What was Wentworth doing here?"

"He came to see me."

"You don't seem too upset about it."

She shrugged. "No, I'm not."

He frowned, examining her expressionless face. "I'm glad to see it didn't affect you, but you didn't have to go that far to prove a point. That *is* why you went to lunch with him, isn't it?"

"Well . . . I don't see any point in holding a grudge."

"After what he tried to do to you?" Darcy looked at her incredulously.

"Marshall's been spoiled all his life. He doesn't always use good judgment," she answered lamely.

"I don't believe this! Are you making excuses for the little thug?"

169

"No, I—I just understand him, that's all."

"Well, maybe you'll explain him to me! The guy almost raped you, and you're telling me he's misunderstood?"

Glory glanced apprehensively around the room. The others all had their heads bent over their desks, but they couldn't help hearing Darcy's raised voice.

"Darcy, please," she murmured.

He gave a smothered exclamation. Grabbing her by the wrist, he pulled her after him into the storeroom.

"Okay, let's have it," he ordered. "I want to know why you're changing your tune all of a sudden."

"I'm not," she insisted. "I just don't see any reason to carry on a vendetta."

"That sure isn't the way you talked the morning after you left him. You couldn't wait to get your freedom."

"I'd just been through a traumatic experience—the accident and everything," she explained haltingly.

"It's the 'everything' I'm talking about," Darcy said grimly. "You were a basket case when I suggested going back to pick up your clothes."

"It was a bad scene," she admitted. She couldn't do anything else. "Marshall is . . . difficult . . . when he's been drinking."

"I don't see any great improvement when he's sober," Darcy replied sardonically. "I deserve the Nobel Peace Prize for not rearranging his ugly features."

"Marshall is very insecure," Glory said placatingly. "He read that article in the paper. You can understand how it would affect him."

"Are you asking me to feel *sorry* for him?"

"No, just to understand."

Glory's nails bit into her damp palms as she realized the impossibility of what she was asking. How could she expect Darcy to accept the unthinkable? Only the real reason would explain it, and she couldn't give him that.

170

"I'm afraid you lost me somewhere along the line." Darcy's face set sternly.

"I told you what it does to him to be held up as an object of ridicule."

"Yeah, he goes out and finds himself a compliant woman," Darcy said disgustedly.

Glory looked down at her twisting fingers. "It doesn't mean anything, though."

Her jerked her chin up. "Are you trying to tell me you didn't care?"

Her long lashes feathered her cheeks. "It wasn't always easy to take, but I realized that I was partly responsible."

"Is that what he told you?" Darcy's steely fingers bit into the soft skin of her upper arms. "I should have taken him apart when I had the chance! Listen to me, my dearest love. Your former husband is a defective human being. Nobody likes rejection, but normal people handle it the way they handle other problems, like income taxes or a leaky roof. You're not responsible because he never developed beyond the tantrum stage in nursery school."

Glory gazed up at the man she loved. Pain slashed through her as she realized once again what she was giving up. "You're so strong, Darcy." She sighed.

He folded her in his arms, brushing his lips across her forehead. "No, sweetheart, I'm just an adult male— something every man should be by the time he reaches his thirties."

Glory gave herself a long moment of experiencing the inexpressible joy of feeling his hard body against hers, the wonderful scent of him in her nostrils. It would have to last her for the rest of her life.

She pulled back reluctantly. "Some men need help to grow up."

Darcy's lean body was suddenly tense. "I get the feeling you're trying to tell me something."

—When she was actually faced with it, Glory waffled. "Everything you said about Marshall is true, but he isn't all bad."

Darcy's eyes narrowed. "I must have missed his good points. Perhaps you can clue me in."

"Well, he . . . he loves me."

"We seem to have a different definition of *love*. What do you call that thing between you and me?" Darcy demanded.

"I'll always be grateful to you, Darcy," she began carefully. "You came along at a difficult time in my life."

He swore under his breath. "I told you I didn't want gratitude. And don't try to tell me that's what you feel for me. I've seen how you react in my arms, Glory; I've heard you beg me to take you. There's never been a sweeter sound than my name on your lips as I brought you joy."

She forced down the memory of their passion. Maybe someday she'd be able to relive those earth-shattering moments, but not now. Dear God, not now! "We were good together," she admitted, choosing her words carefully.

"Were, Glory?"

"As you pointed out, we're all adults now. We have to look to the future. Only children have the luxury of doing exactly what feels best."

"Are you saying Wentworth can provide more toys?" Darcy asked contemptuously. When she looked up at him with misery-filled eyes, he groaned and reached for her. "I'm sorry, sweetheart! That dirty rat fouls everyone he touches, even indirectly."

Glory held him off. It was time to end the agony. "The fact that you said it means it was in the back of your mind. And maybe you're right. Is it so terrible to want some of the material things out of life? Marshall gave me a taste of luxury. After living without it these past weeks, I . . . I find I miss it."

"How about what goes with it?"

She concentrated on the top button of his shirt. "I can handle Marshall."

Darcy's face was like granite. "You're going back to him?"

"Yes." She forced herself not to flinch from the contempt in his eyes.

"Now I know why you wouldn't let me announce our engagement. You gambled that Wentworth might want you back. But if that didn't work out, I was the consolation prize." Darcy shook his head in deep disgust. "You could have made a fortune as an actress if you'd wanted to work for money instead of marrying it. When I think of all those nights you spent in my arms declaring your undying love—I realize now I should have applauded."

A vivid flash of memory reminded Glory of those nights—of the exultant cries of love as Darcy had carried her over the brink with his thrusting masculinity. Why did he persist in reminding her?

She drew a deep breath. "I'm sorry if you feel betrayed. But recriminations aren't going to get you anything but satisfaction, and we have other things to discuss."

"I think we've covered everything," he said austerely.

"I'll stay for a week to train someone to take over my job," she continued.

A vein throbbed at Darcy's temple. "That won't be necessary."

"Unfortunately, it *is* necessary. I confirm your appointments, I coordinate all the activities of the staff so they don't cover the same territory, I take messages and follow up to see that calls are returned. Without someone to direct everything to the right channel, there would be chaos around here." Glory squared her slender shoulders. "In spite of what you think, I do care what happens to you, but I'll leave if you say so."

Darcy frowned. He fought a silent battle with himself, then said grudgingly, "I suppose it would create a problem. Okay, find somebody to take over—*fast!*"

She could almost feel her heart cracking in tiny pieces at the look of betrayal in his eyes. If Darcy only knew it, the next week would be worse punishment than her lifetime sentence with Marshall.

Glory was too listless to do anything but sink down on the couch when she got home that night. She sat there in the gathering darkness, trying to make her mind a blank. Otherwise she would have to face the terrible shambles her life had become. The doorbell forced her to return to reality. Glory hurriedly switched on some lamps before answering the door.

Ellen raised her eyebrows at Glory's skirt and blouse. "You haven't even started to get ready yet?"

"Ready for what?"

"The big rally at Civic Center," Ellen said impatiently. "Celebrities, movie stars—does that ring a bell? We've only been talking about it all week!"

Glory, quite understandably, had forgotten. "Oh . . . yes, of course. I'm not going, though."

"You're kidding! You said this was one of the few fun events on the circuit. Short speeches and lots of entertainment."

"Yes, but I—I have a headache."

"Take some aspirin."

"That won't help," Glory answered somberly.

Ellen looked at her more closely. "You do look kind of ragged. Are you coming down with something?"

"It's possible," Glory said, since it seemed the easiest thing to say. Ellen would want to hear the whole story if she told her the truth, and Glory knew she couldn't go through it again.

"Gee, that's a shame. Darcy will be so disappointed. Does he know you're not going?"

"Yes, he knows. Hadn't you better be getting ready?" It was a tactful way to get rid of her. Glory's nerves were at the breaking point.

"I have a few minutes yet. Can I fix you anything? Some hot tea, maybe?"

The phone rang as Glory was shaking her head. She clutched the receiver tightly when Marshall's voice greeted her.

"How did it go today when you got back to the office?" he asked.

"None of your damn business," she snapped.

"That bad, huh?" He laughed.

"What do you want?"

"Is that any way to talk to a man who's counting the hours until he has his wife back again?"

"Listen to me." Glory's voice was measured and deadly. "We agreed on one week. For the next seven days I don't expect to see you or hear from you. Is that clear?" She hung up without waiting for an answer.

Ellen whistled. "Wow! Who was that?"

"Nobody important," Glory replied grimly.

"It sounded like a bill collector."

"I guess you could call him that." Glory's eyes were shadowed. "I'd almost forgotten about an old debt, but it suddenly became due."

"He wants payment immediately?"

"In a week," Glory murmured. "I just hope I can make it!" The words were torn out of her.

"That's really tough. I don't know how deeply you're in hock, but I have some money put aside. You're welcome to it," Ellen offered.

Glory was touched by her generous offer. She and Ellen hadn't even known each other that long. "Thanks, but I don't need money," she said gently.

"You just said you were in a bind." Ellen looked bewildered.

"No, I—What I meant was, I can get it."

"I realize Darcy would give it to you. He'd do anything for you. I just thought maybe you'd prefer not to ask him." Ellen grinned. "We don't have to tell men *all* our secrets."

"No, there are some things we have to keep from them," Glory said slowly. She managed a little smile. "You'd better get dressed, or there will be two handsome bachelors without dates."

"I'll keep an eye on Darcy for you," Ellen promised. "Although that's about as necessary as an ice machine is to an Eskimo. I never saw a man so dotty over a woman."

Glory moved toward the door, hoping Ellen would take the hint.

Ellen followed, but she wasn't finished with the subject. "Even if I hadn't fallen in love with Bryan and seen the light, I think Darcy might have changed my opinion of men. He's almost too good to be true. I've watched women tripping each other to get to him, but he can't see anyone but you. And the way he treats you! It's a revelation."

Every word went through Glory like a knife. When Ellen paused for agreement she murmured, "Bryan cares that much about you."

Ellen laughed. "Did it sound like I was after your fiancé? Don't worry. I was just expressing overdue admiration. Bryan is my real love." She sighed happily. "I can't conceive of a life without him."

After she finally left, Glory leaned against the door and closed her eyes wearily. She could tell Ellen what life was like without the man you loved. Would it always hurt this much, or would time dull the pain? Glory was afraid she already knew the answer to that.

CHAPTER ELEVEN

The week that followed was the disaster Glory expected it to be. Darcy avoided her as much as possible, but when he was forced to speak to her he was coldly polite. Besides being shattering, it was embarrassing.

Darcy had made no secret of his feelings for her before. The fact that Glory wouldn't let him announce their engagement hadn't made him the least bit circumspect. He was not only openly affectionate but possessive as well. Everyone took it for granted that they were just waiting for the election to be over before being married.

Now the people in the office were uncomfortable. They guessed there had been an argument, but they couldn't know its magnitude. George and Gretchen and all the rest waited for it to blow over. It made for a sticky situation when it didn't.

Darcy was the heart of the whole operation. He was the conductor who got the best out of them by leading the way. The office had always been a happy, boisterous place because he was in charge. He was cheerful and confident, instilling the same qualities in everyone else. Now all that was changed. Darcy had become as remote as a mountain peak.

Bryan was the only one who tried to do something about it. He had grown more and more worried as the gloom thickened. One morning he stopped by Glory's desk.

"Let's go out for coffee," he suggested.

"Sally just made a fresh pot," she told him.

"I feel like some fresh air. Walk down to the snack shop with me." He smiled appealingly. "If we leave some campaign literature, we can justify it on the expense account."

Glory had a pretty good idea of what was on his mind, and it wasn't something she was prepared to discuss. "I really have a lot to do, Bryan."

"I'll buy you a jelly doughnut," he offered hopefully.

Through the glass partition, Glory saw Darcy get up from his desk. She had no reason to think he was coming to speak to her, but she decided not to take the chance. "Okay, I suddenly got hungry," she told Bryan.

A few minutes later, when they were seated at the counter with their coffee, he didn't waste time beating around the bush. "What's wrong between you and Darcy?"

Glory stirred her coffee, looking into the swirling depths. "Don't you think that's rather personal?"

"In other words, mind my own business?" he asked ruefully.

"I wouldn't put it exactly that way," she answered carefully.

"You'd be justified if you did, but I'm not some nosey neighbor. I'm very fond of you, Glory, and you know how I feel about Darcy."

"If you care about him, leave it alone, Bryan," she said dully.

"You don't mean that! You've had an argument, but it isn't worth breaking up over."

"People do it all the time. Nothing is forever."

"You and Darcy are," he said confidently. "I've experienced the kind of love you two share, and I'm fortunate enough to have found it again; so I know what I'm talking about."

"There's a greater kind of love," Glory murmured,

gazing into her cup as she tried to feel noble—and felt only despair.

Bryan's forehead wrinkled. "I don't understand."

She pulled herself together. It was dangerous to indulge in self-pity. "Darcy and I are attracted to each other physically. For a while it was enough, but it isn't anymore," she said crisply.

"I can't believe that's all there was," he protested.

"Because you don't want to. You and Ellen have something entirely different going, so you're seeing the world through a pink haze. Not every story has a happy ending." Glory's voice was flat.

"You're trying to tell me you didn't have an argument?"

She sighed. "Most affairs break up with an argument."

Bryan frowned. "It's too bad Darcy can't take it as philosophically as you."

"He'll get over it." Glory knew how callous that sounded by Bryan's grim expression. He couldn't guess how much worse it was for her.

"I hope it'll be soon," Bryan remarked austerely. "He isn't doing his career any good lately."

"Things will look up in a few days," she assured him. "I'll be leaving next Thursday."

Glory went back to the office, realizing she'd lost a friend. About the only ones she hadn't alienated so far were Ellen and Mrs. Belmont, Glory reflected bleakly.

The days that used to fly by now dragged on like years. Glory wasn't sleeping well and food held no interest. She lost a couple of pounds in just a few days, weight that her already slender body couldn't afford. She was always tired, too.

One day when she was swamped with a seemingly endless amount of paperwork, Glory put her head back and closed her eyes for a moment. She opened them with the feeling that someone was staring at her. Darcy stood by the desk, surveying her with a frown.

A muscle twitched in his taut jaw. "It didn't take Wentworth long to put you back in the same state I found you in."

Glory knew the sleepless nights had taken their toll. It was small consolation that Darcy looked haggard, too. His high cheekbones were more prominent, and there were deep lines from his nose to his taut mouth— the mouth that used to be so full and sensuous against hers. Glory lowered her lashes quickly.

"Did you want something?" she murmured.

"Yes, I want to talk to you. Come into my office," he said curtly.

She followed slowly, tensing herself for more condemnation. But Darcy surprised her.

When the door was closed he said, "I want to apologize for the things I said the other day. They were inexcusable."

It was the last thing she expected. "I . . . That's all right. I understand."

"You're very forgiving." He stared at her moodily, examining the delicate contours of her lovely face. "Don't do it, Glory!" he said abruptly. "If you've decided you don't love me, that's one thing; but don't throw yourself away on a reject like Wentworth."

Her head drooped. "We've been all through this, Darcy."

"I don't understand." He raked his fingers through his thick dark hair. "Look at you! You look like a walking disaster victim. Don't tell me you're going back to him because you love the guy. I don't believe it! And I don't believe you're doing it for money either. So what is it?"

Glory was fiercely glad that Darcy had changed his opinion of her, but it presented a problem. "Marshall needs me," she offered lamely.

"Not as much as I do." Darcy's hands cupped her neck. His thumb made a slow circle over the wildly beating pulse at the base of her throat. "It was so good between us, sweetheart. Remember?"

How could she forget? His lean body was only inches from hers, a reminder of the ecstasy it could bring. Glory clenched her fists tightly to keep from moving into his arms.

"I've given my word," she said tonelessly. "I can't go back on it."

His hands tightened unconsciously on her neck. "How about your promise to me?"

"I wasn't free to give it. I'm still married to Marshall."

"Is there some problem with the divorce? All you have to do is tell me about it. I'm a lawyer, honey. I can fix it."

His softened tone was almost her undoing. Glory felt tears clog her throat as she gazed into his concerned face. Darcy was so loving. He would do anything for her, but this was something she had to fix herself.

"I'm going back to Marshall," she stated flatly. "Nothing you or anyone else can say will change my mind. You'll just have to accept it."

"Not until you give me the real reason." Darcy's eyes narrowed. "What hold does he have over you?"

Fear shot through Glory. She forced herself to return his gaze steadily. "Now you're being melodramatic. I know it would make you feel better to think I'm an unwilling victim, but it just isn't so. I know exactly what I'm doing." She could feel his eyes burning into her back as she turned and left the room.

Glory didn't know if she could keep up the fiction if Darcy continued to chip away at her defenses. She was already on the ragged edge, loving him so much it was an actual ache. One more reminder of the rapture they'd shared might make her ruin his life. Her salva-

181

tion came in the form of a phone call from Marshall's grandmother.

"I would have called you sooner, my dear, but Marshall wouldn't tell me where to find you," the old lady complained. "I do think you might have called *me.*"

"I . . . I'm sorry, Mrs. Wentworth. I didn't know if you'd want to hear from me."

"You didn't want a scolding—that's what you mean! And that's what you would have gotten. I realize I'm an old woman living in the past, but I can't say these new-fangled ways make much sense. Finding yourself, indeed! As though a person could lose herself!"

"I don't understand." Glory was puzzled by the seeming gibberish since Marshall's grandmother had always been exceedingly sharp.

"It's all very well to get a job if you feel you want to do something worthwhile. I quite approve of that. You always were a smart girl, Glory. But separate dwellings is simply carrying things too far. I'm glad you finally came to your senses and decided to return home where you belong."

A glimmer of light started to penetrate. "What exactly did Marshall tell you?" Glory asked cautiously.

"The whole story—after I insisted. But don't worry. I didn't give him any sympathy. I told him if he wasn't man enough to keep his wife happy, he couldn't complain if she went out and found something more exciting to do. After all, you did take a job instead of merely frittering your time away. Not that I approve, but it doesn't hurt to shake that young man up a bit." The elderly woman gave a raspy chuckle. "I told him he was lucky you didn't leave him permanently."

"I see," Glory replied slowly. Marshall had obviously been afraid to tell his grandmother the truth. That was the reason he kept her away from Glory. The old lady had a rigid code of morals. If Glory told her side of the story, Marshall might be cut out of her will.

"Well, what's past is past," Mrs. Wentworth was continuing. "What I called for is to find out if you really want that boat Marshall asked me for."

"Boat?" Glory asked blankly.

"A cabin cruiser, I believe he called it. He says it sleeps eight, but I can't imagine the accommodations would be very luxurious. Does it appeal to you, my dear?"

"It sounds expensive," Glory said doubtfully.

"Who else do I have to spend my money on? The only way I'll buy it, though, is if you two will enjoy it together."

Glory knew this was just Marshall's latest whim. But if it made him happy, he might be easier to live with. "Thank you, Mrs. Wentworth." She tried to put appreciation in her voice. "A cabin cruiser would be a wonderful gift."

A sound made Glory look up. Darcy was standing there with such disgust in his blazing eyes that she flinched.

"I just got my answer," he grated. "It isn't Marshall's piddling little money you're after. You're going for the whole family fortune! Too bad I didn't have enough assets to bid for you. I like the way you show your gratitude."

Glory gazed after his stiff retreating back with stricken eyes. Their brief détente had ended in an ugly bang. It was for the best of course, but she was too crushed to appreciate it.

The receiver made squawking noises in her clenched hand. "Glory! Glory! What happened to you, child?"

It was the evening of that same traumatic day that Ellen decided to add her voice to all the others.

Glory had been avoiding her all week in order to avert just such an encounter. Bryan would undoubtedly have told her that Darcy and she had broken up, and

Glory didn't want to explain. She had parried all of Ellen's questions, mostly by changing the subject or saying she had somewhere to go. They hadn't spent more than a few minutes together at a time.

That evening when Glory answered the door, she could tell that Ellen was going to demand some answers. It couldn't have come at a worse time.

Ellen confirmed her suspicions by walking right in. "I know you don't want to talk about the fight you had with Darcy, but maybe it would help. Sometimes a third person can put things in perspective."

Glory mustered a wan smile. "Thanks, but I already have twenty-twenty vision."

"Not if you're prepared to give up a man like Darcy. I don't know what the argument was about, but it can't be that important. Look what it's doing to you! Make up with him before you waste away to a shadow."

"I can't," Glory whispered.

"What's wrong with you two?" Ellen exclaimed impatiently. "Bryan says Darcy snaps at everyone like a Great Dane with the gout, and you're about as cheerful as a weeping willow, but neither of you will forget your silly pride."

"It'll all be over soon," Glory replied, sighing heavily.

"It had better be! I was prepared to lock you in a room together and keep you there until you talked this out."

"I'm going back to Marshall," Glory announced quietly.

Ellen looked as though she hadn't heard correctly. "You're kidding me, aren't you?"

"No, I'm giving up my apartment next Thursday."

"But *why,* for God's sake? After all the things you told me about him?"

"I can't tell you that, Ellen. Please don't ask me," Glory begged. "Just accept it. Darcy has."

"If you think I'm going to let you throw away your life without even knowing the reason, you're crazier than you're acting right now!"

Glory put her hands over her ears. "Why doesn't everyone leave me alone? Can't you see what you're doing to me? I can't take anymore!"

Ellen looked shaken. "I'm sorry. I didn't realize . . ." She hesitated. "Is there anything I can do?"

Tears welled up in Glory's green eyes. "Just don't think too badly of me. Everyone hates me, but you know I wouldn't do the things they're imagining if I had any choice."

Ellen led her to the couch. "Don't you think you'd feel better if you told me about it?" she asked gently.

A dam seemed to burst inside Glory. She talked on and on, explaining, looking again for loopholes that weren't there, grieving over the fact. Ellen listened without interrupting. She let her get it all out of her system.

Then she said quietly, "You can't go through with it. You have to tell Darcy."

Glory shook her head. "You know what he would do: he'd pull out of the race."

"No! He'd stand up and fight, which is what you should be doing."

"I would if it didn't threaten Darcy's future. I don't care what they say about *me!* But I won't pull him down with me."

"He won't ever forgive you if he finds out you didn't trust him enough to make his own decision," Ellen warned.

"He thinks the worst of me already," Glory replied hopelessly. "If he's going to despise me, it might as well be in a good cause."

"That's about the fuzziest thinking I've ever heard," Ellen said disgustedly. "If you're too dumb to take charge of your own life, I'm going to do it for you."

"No!" Glory's body tensed instantly. "I want your

sacred promise that you won't say a word to Darcy about this!"

"But, Glory, don't you see—"

"Promise me!" Glory demanded adamantly.

In the end, Ellen had to give in. Glory was wound so tightly that she was actually afraid for her. Ellen went back to her own apartment with deep misgivings.

As the allotted week drew to a close, Glory grew fatalistic. On the final Thursday she was almost calm. The woman she had trained for her job was working out well, and Darcy had been out of the office all day. He probably wanted to avoid painful good-byes as much as she did. What was there left to say?

Still, Glory felt a pang as she cleaned out her desk. She would never see him again except in the newspapers or on television.

Ellen was waiting for her when she got home. The determination on her face warned that she was going to make one final plea, but Glory didn't let it bother her. She was in a numbed state.

When Ellen followed her inside without being asked, Glory said, "You'll have to come in the bedroom with me. I have to pack."

Ellen watched her take lingerie out of drawers. "Do you think it's cricket to wear the nightgowns Darcy bought you when you go to bed with Marshall?" she asked in a conversational tone of voice.

Glory crushed the fragile garment tightly. "That's remarkably crude," she replied coldly.

Ellen's eyes were on Glory's clenched hands. "It's one of the facts of life. Husbands and wives do sleep together." When Glory didn't answer, she went on, "I suppose you haven't wanted to think about that. I know *I* wouldn't, after what you've told me."

Unwanted memories rose up to choke Glory. She

turned pale and sank down on the bed as her legs suddenly gave way.

"It isn't too late to back out," Ellen said urgently. "I'll stay here to give you moral support when he comes."

Glory bent her head, fighting down nausea. "Go home, Ellen." Her voice was faint, but it left no room for argument.

Ellen's mouth was grim as she slammed the door of her own apartment. She stalked to the telephone and looked down at it balefully. "If I die in hell for breaking a sacred promise, I'm going to come back and stick you with a pitchfork, Glory Prescott!" she muttered as she picked up the receiver and quickly dialed a familiar number.

"Yes, Ellen, what can I do for you?" Darcy asked a moment later. He was trying to sound cordial—and failing miserably.

"I have to talk to you about Glory."

His affability fled. "I'm sorry, but that's one thing I don't care to discuss."

"I think you'd better listen to me," Ellen stated firmly.

After she had finished, the lines disappeared magically from Darcy's face. A look of wonder softened his rugged features. "She would do a thing like that for me?"

"It's going to be an accomplished fact if you don't get over here fast!"

"Don't worry. I'll take care of everything." Darcy hung up the phone and rose to his feet like a boxer spoiling to get into the ring. His eyes gleamed and the smile on his face looked like a permanent fixture.

Marshall stood in the middle of the living room, glancing around Glory's charming apartment. "So this is what you traded a big house in Beverly Hills for—a bunch of used furniture in a second-rate part of town."

She didn't bother to answer the taunt. "I'm almost through packing. You can sit down and wait."

He followed her into the bedroom instead. "At least it's got a big enough bed. How about trying it out before we say good-bye to this dump?"

"Those boxes are ready to be carried out." Her voice was impersonal.

Marshall laughed. "What's the matter, baby? Still sulking about losing your boyfriend? I guess I'll just have to find some way to keep you amused."

"On your new boat?" she asked sardonically.

His smug smile was replaced by a wary expression. "What do you know about that?"

"Your grandmother called me."

He grabbed her arm roughly. "What did you tell her?"

"What she told *me* was more interesting." Glory jerked her arm away. "Apparently you're not the only one in possession of a damaging little secret. All this time I thought you'd been served with divorce papers— isn't that strange?"

"Grandmother always liked you," Marshall said placatingly. "I didn't want to hurt her."

"Sell that story to television. I hear they'll buy anything," Glory hooted.

"Okay, so I didn't tell her—and you won't either! As far as she knows, we're happily married."

"Nobody is *that* good an actress," she replied contemptuously.

He moved menacingly close. "I'm warning you, Glory—" The doorbell cut off Marshall's threat.

She went to answer the door, hoping it wasn't Ellen. Her good intentions would only make a hopeless situation worse. When Glory saw Darcy standing on the threshold instead, she turned pale.

Glory knew she was in the midst of some kind of dream when he smiled charmingly and bent his head to kiss her trembling mouth.

"Hello, sweetheart." He cupped her cheek, gazing into her eyes with deep emotion. "It's good to have you back."

Marshall had followed Glory into the living room. His face was ugly as he watched the tender scene. "That happens to be my wife you're pawing."

"Your *ex*-wife," Darcy stated firmly. "Glory is going to marry me."

"Oh, yeah? Ask her!" Marshall gloated.

"I told you I was going back to Marshall," she whispered pleadingly.

"But you didn't tell me you were being blackmailed into it." Darcy took her icy fingers in his warm hands. "Do you think I'd ever let you do a thing like that?"

"Save the pretty speeches for the campaign trail," Marshall snapped. "Glory comes back to me, or you can kiss that state senate seat good bye. How do you think the voters would feel about a candidate who was having an affair with a married woman? The newspapers would eat it up."

"He's right, Darcy. You can't—" Glory began urgently.

"Let me handle this, darling." Darcy's voice had a ring of steel as he turned to the other man. "As long as we're trying this case in the papers, let's bring in all the evidence—like the fact that she ran away because you attempted to rape her."

"Are you crazy? We were married!" Marshall shouted indignantly.

"The courts recognize a case of rape if one partner is unwilling, regardless of marital status," Darcy pointed out with satisfaction. "I think people would also be interested in the events leading up to the assault. Infidelity makes such juicy reading."

"You're bluffing," Marshall snarled. "It would cause a stink that would blow you right out of the race!"

Darcy shrugged. "If you circulate your lies to the gossip columnists, I won't have a career in politics anyhow. This way I get to take you down with me."

"I won't say anything if Glory comes back to me," Marshall said uncertainly.

"She isn't going to." Darcy's eyes were icy. "Now, do you slink out of here like the rodent you are, or do I beat the hell out of you and call the papers myself?"

Glory could almost see Marshall's mind working frantically. Fear mixed with hatred as he sought desperately for a way to save his skin—both literally and figuratively.

Finally he sneered, "If it means that much to you, take her! I wouldn't want her back after you had her anyway." Marshall moved swiftly out the door before Darcy could get his hands on him.

"Let him go." Glory grabbed Darcy's arm.

He hesitated, torn two ways. Then his clenched fists slowly uncurled. "I guess you're right. He isn't worth a murder rap, which is surely what I'd commit if I ever caught him."

Glory's face wore a dazed expression. "I can't believe it's over."

Darcy took her in his arms and buried her head against his solid shoulder. "It must have been hell for you, sweetheart."

"The worst part was having you think all those terrible things about me. But there wasn't any other way." She pleaded for understanding.

"I knew they weren't true," he said soothingly. "That's what drove me crazy—that and losing you." He stroked her hair lovingly. "Don't you know you're all that matters to me?"

"Would you really have let Marshall ruin you?" she asked uncertainly.

"In a minute." He kissed her gently. "What good is a career if you're not there to share it?"

When Glory realized there was nothing to prevent it now, a fountain of happiness started to bubble inside her. "You don't know what you let yourself in for. I'm going to stick to you like adhesive tape, night and day!"

"A verbal agreement is binding, but I wouldn't mind a show of good faith." Darcy's arms crossed over her hips, drawing Glory's lower body against his.

She gazed up at him through long lashes. "What do you think would be suitable?"

"I had total possession in mind," he answered huskily.

Lifting her into his arms, he carried her into the bedroom. He joined her on the bed without letting her out of his grasp. While his lips covered hers, his hands wandered over her body in a slow journey of remembrance.

Glory quivered as his fingers lighted smoldering fires. Her breasts swelled under his lingering touch, and when he bent his head to nip at the hardened peaks through her blouse, she raked her fingers through his hair with a wordless cry.

Darcy's tawny eyes blazed as he slowly undressed her. He kissed every inch of her satin skin, starting at her shoulders and ending with her thighs. Flames erupted wherever his burning mouth paused, until Glory was a fluid mass of desire.

"I need you so, darling," she gasped, tugging the shirt out of his slacks.

"We need each other, love of my life," he answered huskily.

He flung off his clothes and returned to kneel over her. Glory caressed his body as he had caressed hers, running her hands over his hard chest and taut stomach, down to the proof of his passion.

With a hoarse cry Darcy clasped her to him, filling Glory with remembered ecstasy. His driving force was deeply satisfying. She arched her body into his again and again, meeting his male challenge with joy. They climbed to dizzying heights together and reached the summit at the same time.

Lightning bolts shot through Glory's body, severing the tension and leaving throbbing waves of sensation in its place. They diminished and grew farther apart, until only gentle vibrations were left. Her taut body relaxed against Darcy's, and they clung together in total peace.

Their fulfillment was so great that neither stirred for a long time. Finally he started to stroke her back with sated enjoyment. Glory made an appreciative little sound, doing the same to him.

"Will you mind living in Sacramento part-time if I win the election?" he asked idly.

She scraped her nails lightly up his spine. "What do you mean *if*, Mr. Senator?"

He chuckled. "That's what I like: confidence. You haven't answered my question, though."

Glory put her arms around his neck, gazing at him with pure love. "Don't you know I'd follow you anywhere? I'm your most loyal constituent."

Darcy fitted her body more firmly to his. "I like the way you cast your vote," he murmured.